ALETTA THORNE

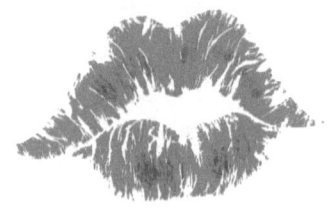

EVERNIGHT PUBLISHING ®

www.evernightpublishing.com

Copyright© 2018

Aletta Thorne

Editor: Lisa Petrocelli

Cover Artist: Jay Aheer

ISBN: 978-1-77339-575-3

ALETTA THORNE

DEDICATION

To everyone who swore she saw something out of the corner of her eye. And to the something she saw.

ALETTA THORNE

THE CHEF AND THE GHOST OF BARTHOLOMEW ADDISON JENKINS

Aletta Thorne

Copyright © 2017

Chapter One

October, 1982

As she considered stuffing the dripping wet wire pot scrubber down the front of her chef's whites, Alma wondered if her mother was right. Maybe she *was* wasting her life—or at least, her English degree.

But you did what paid the bills, and being a poet certainly wasn't an option. Besides, she hadn't written a thing in years. So Alma became a chef—not formally trained, but every bit good as many who were. She'd worked in shouty, sweaty restaurants, but her new job was a sweet one—running the kitchen at a private residential center for kids with emotional trouble.

Bright Day School was housed on a pleasantly out-at-the-elbows Tudor-style estate overlooking the Hudson River in upstate New York. It sprawled over a cluster of old buildings with stucco walls and dark woodwork. Its students, despite the scary-sounding names of their problems, turned out to be lots like other kids—heartbreaking, funny, and in need of a good meal. Alma was happy to help out with that last thing. She ran a peaceful kitchen, and she wasn't too proud to wash her own pots. Hence the scrubber.

   She'd been having a fun day, too ... until her sous chef, Jessie, spotted a certain dinged-up green Ford Capri backing into a parking space outside the main building's leaded glass kitchen windows. The Capri was owned by one of Alma's least favorite gentleman callers—Charlie Sassian, of the County Health Department.

   Dammit, dammit, dammit! Alma squeezed the wire pot scrubber in her hand. She knew the thing was totally, completely, get-you-in-trouble illegal—but also kind of necessary. A steel scrubber was, for example, the only way to get the scorched remains of Szechuan chicken in orange sauce off the bottom of the giant roasting pan she'd just used as a wok. It had been *tasty* Szechuan chicken in orange sauce, too! Excellent, really.

   During the last inspection, Alma had gotten written up for chucking a wire scrubber just like it into an open garbage can. Charlie Sassian had spotted it the second he walked in the door. The man was capable of peering into the trash before he even said hello. Now he was looking over some papers on his clipboard, and slamming his car door. Once burned, twice shy. Into Alma's bra went the prickly, wet scrubber. It felt awful immediately.

   Plus now, she smelled like garlic and ginger. *Delicious!*

   Alma tightened her apron over her newly lopsided shirt. "Well, *fuck*," she said quietly, to no one in particular. On the other side of the stainless steel prep table, Jessie tucked a few stray brown curls back into her purple silk scarf. Alma nervously checked her toque for any of her own unruly blonde hair. Then, the back door to the kitchen swung open, and in walked Charlie with his stupid baggy tweed jacket over his neatly ironed pink polo shirt and baggy chinos. Charlie the garbage can spy. Charlie with his fussy instant-read thermometer, used mostly to make sure anyone feeding kids in large numbers cooked everything to the consistency of antique cardboard.

He had to be a year or two older than her—in his mid-thirties, perhaps. His dark red hair was rubber-banded into a long, messy pigtail. *There really is nothing attractive about that man.* Alma turned her warmest smile on him. The pot scrubber itched. A lot.

"Alma!" he said, extending a pale freckled hand. "Good to see you again!" *Hmm. He ignored the garbage this time. Shoulda stashed the scrubber in there again.* They shook hands and right afterward, without thinking, Alma wiped her fingers on the towel she kept looped into her apron.

"Oh … um … sorry," she said. "*That* was rude!" She giggled nervously, and Charlie didn't laugh with her. "Want a cup of coffee?"

His eyes darted around the kitchen before settling on hers again. "Not just now. Perhaps in a *non-*professional setting, though," he said and then he smiled. "My treat. Sometime soon?" *Ugh.* This was a new twist. Jessie scampered into the room with the giant KitchenAid mixer and the slicing machine, her lips tight, barely containing a fit of her own giggles.

"Ah, Charlie," Alma said. "You know I've only been here a month. New job. I have *no* time to socialize. So, let me show you what we did downstairs in the walk-in cooler. I think we've fixed everything. The new shelves are the ones you suggested…"

As she walked down the stairs with Charlie following her, Alma felt moist bits of orange chicken scrapings fall off the scrubber and land on her stomach. Thank God she'd gotten the cartons of lettuce and oranges the co-op had just delivered up off the floor and *onto* those new shelves! And thank God, too, that Benny the Beemer, their junior vocational trainee, had finished running the dish machine and was safely back in class for the afternoon.

Benny the Beemer made race car noises pretty much all the time, hence his nickname. No one was supposed to use it, everyone did anyway, and that made Benny very happy. Alma often forgot to tell him that imitating BMW 507s instead of actually talking to people was *inappropriate*. *Inappropriate* was the word she'd been firmly instructed to use when the kids who worked in the kitchen acted out their symptoms. A visit from the Department of Health would have gotten some braking and cornering squeals out of Benny, for sure. Alma flicked on the lights in the walk-in and enjoyed that idea.

Charlie walked in behind her. "Okay. Not too bad," he said.

Bright Day School was owned by a family of cheerful and very well-off hippies who believed that good food was therapeutic. They'd hired Alma away from Alberto's, the restaurant at the local winery. The wine there was beyond terrible, but the food was great, and Alma was proud of that. Alma's theory about her new job? Her old clientele wasn't so different from the kids and staff she fed at Bright Day. The people who'd eaten at the winery just hadn't been diagnosed … *yet.*

Bright Day School was also where almost everyone single Alma's age in Engelhook-on-Hudson worked. There were plenty of jobs for social workers, therapists, child care workers, and teachers. Plus a full staff of kitchen workers for Alma to manage. Engelhook was a newly hip upstate New York town, a really good place for her to have landed. Plenty of pretty old houses with cheap rent. Alma lived in one of those, and she liked it—lots. Please, she thought, as Charlie poked into her cartons and under her shelves. *No violations this time! I really need this job!*

She'd only been cooking for a paycheck for two years, ever since she'd walked out on the hard-drinking painter and professor her parents still adored. Alma's folks were profs, too. Her mom in film, her dad in English. Alma had been together on and off with Stefan Rauch most of her senior year at New Paltz. They'd gotten married the week she graduated.

Stefan was ten years Alma's senior, with a shaggy head of curly black hair lately going grey at the temples. His loft apartment had white brick walls covered with his huge super-realistic paintings of abandoned industrial sites. Twenty perfectly folded black t-shirts were all he had in his dresser, no other clothes except for his jeans and a black leather jacket. Stefan didn't believe in underwear any more than he believed in abstract art. He spent way more time in front of a canvas than any other painter he knew, painstakingly rendering the exact play of light on rusted steel and broken glass. Working that hard made him permanently angry.

As a newlywed, Alma couldn't believe she actually got to live in a place like Stefan's loft. She couldn't believe she got to write poetry instead of going to a day job. Stefan had insisted upon that. No selling out allowed! He also believed that creative writing graduate programs were stupid.

"It's only words! Do the work yourself!" he said to her from time to time. "Like me! I do *all* the work myself." Except there was a problem. It was impossible for Alma get anything of her own done around Stefan. He got frustrated and bellowed at his paintings. He

11

stormed around the loft on the mornings he had to get up and teach class. He knocked back Budweiser in tall cans the way most people drink coffee. And he and Alma's family had roaring-drunk dinner parties together ... for eight long years.

Alma had finally left him the night she'd come home to a flood. Their big, claw-foot tub was overflowing with bubble bath, and sitting in it with her husband was an impossibly skinny girl with a jet black crew cut. Alma recognized her as one of his undergraduates right away. Ms. Crew Cut was laughing and red-faced—and Stefan was laughing, too. He got out of the tub and splash-walked to the bathroom door, his suddenly ridiculous cock swinging absurdly between his legs.

"Ooops!" he'd said, and popped open a bottle of champagne he'd left beside the sink. "Have a swig, dearest?" The sparkling wine fizzed over his fingers and dripped into with the soapsuds on the floor. Another bottle sat next to the tub, empty.

Although she'd vowed on her graduation day that she would never again sleep a night under her parents' roof, Alma had walked out of Stefan's loft without a word and driven herself back to Briarcliff Manor.

"Men *do* that, honey," her mother had said. "Especially the creative types. Most of them, anyway. It doesn't mean anything, you know. Not a thing! Stefan's such *fun!* Please! Give him another chance." But Alma hadn't. And as she stood in the cooler with Charlie turning over papers on his clipboard, the divorce had been final for two whole weeks. Thanks to Stefan's vicious lawyer and her sweet-but-bumbling one, there had not been one penny of a settlement in it for her.

Fortunately, Alma loved food. She'd collected

cook books since high school. So, she'd learned her way around a professional kitchen. Her first job had been in a health food restaurant in downtown Engelhook. Her old college friend, Mary Connor, had put in a word for her. Mary had grown up in Englehook. She'd studied art and ended up a cook, too. Mary had been Alma's first hire at Bright Day.

Now, Alma stared at a case of Romaine lettuce and prayed the inspection really was going well. Charlie hadn't said anything for a while. She fought the urge to pull the unbearably itchy, ice-cold pot scrubber out of her bra right that very minute. Charlie picked up a carton of apples and ran a finger over clean stainless steel shelving underneath it … and nodded appreciatively.

"*Much* better," he said.

"So you like what you're seeing this time?" said Alma, and immediately regretted putting it that way as she felt his eyes sweep over her.

"Yeah, I do," said Charlie. "Lots. Oh, C'mon, Alma, you can't be *that* busy. Institutional food is easier than your old restaurant gig, right? How about I take you to dinner instead? Hey, I know who's got a clean kitchen, right? Dinner and a movie? I hear *Poltergeist* is at The Apex again. Halloween's coming, you know."

Alma glanced down. Underneath her apron, her shirt was quite wet from the pot scrubber and standing inside a refrigerator didn't make that any more comfortable. "Actually … no. I mean, nothing personal, but my job is my *job* and I don't…"

Charlie winced. "Okay, I get it. I'm sorry. That was out of line, I guess," he said. "Ed said you guys from Alberto's liked to party, though so… Oh, *crap*. That was worse! Open mouth, insert foot." He smacked himself in the forehead. Ed Chaikin was the other inspector, the one Alma had seen in restaurants. "I didn't mean to put you in a bad position. I know you're working very hard. I know—"

"It's okay," said Alma brightly. Charlie truly was kind of a jerk but now she felt sorry for him. There was an awkward silence as she searched for something to say. "Thing about me is that I'm the only person in the world who doesn't really *like* movies, anyway. I'd rather read." That was true. As the daughter of a film professor, she'd seen way too many movies. Especially scary ones. She hated movies with blood and gore, the kind that made you jump. But, her mother worshipped Alfred Hitchcock. Alma was even supposed to have been named after him, except she turned out to be a girl. So her mom named her after Alfred Hitchcock's wife, instead.

"Looks like the violations you had down here have been all seen to," Charlie said. "Please understand that I'm not trying to be a bad guy, Alma. You just have to be super careful with the sanitation when you're feeding kids. It's like hospitals. You've obviously worked your butt off to clean this place up. I see that. I'll have a quick look at the stockroom and be on my way." He sighed and smiled. Funny how he didn't look *quite* so … loathsome, now. But the guy was no prize.

"Want an apple?" said Alma. "They're Winesaps, from Depew's Orchard on 9W. Really good."

Charlie picked one up and followed her upstairs.

Back in the kitchen, Jessie was signing in the night's fish order, and Jan Gleason had arrived for the dinner shift. The Bright Day kitchen usually had one head cook and one prep cook per meal, except for breakfast, which was a solo gig. Alma often did breakfast, sometimes Jess, except on the weekends. Because it was a school kitchen, not a restaurant kitchen, everyone was female—except for Jan. He did dinner five nights a week. A good cook, easy to work with—

although a lot of that had to do with his usual prep, Alma's old friend, Mary.

Jan's biggest attribute was that he was—not to mince words—blindingly gorgeous. Broad shouldered, light brown hair, round glasses with clear plastic rims a lot like the ones John Lennon had worn. Alma didn't even like to admit to herself how much she enjoyed watching Jan work. Jessie would be his prep tonight, lucky girl. Mary was off, and Jessie was working a double. Overtime pay to collect—and tasty eye candy, too!

"Hey, Jan," Alma said to him. "Hold off changing into your whites a sec. Department of Health's here. Charlie Sassian's just finishing the stockroom."

Jan nodded, and then tilted his head.

"No. It's good," whispered Alma. Then she raised her voice. "I got you the fish heads you wanted for the chowder stock," she continued. "Big ones—groupers, I think. I'll make the cornbread before I go. Jess can do up the slaw. Got Winesaps for apple crisp downstairs…" She shivered. To her horror, the pot scrubber's dampness had now soaked through her apron, too, marking the outline of her right breast in a wet circle. She crossed her arms over her chest, and hoped nothing showed.

"Alma? Everything's fine back here," called Charlie. "Just need you to sign this." He appeared next to her with his clipboard.

As she uncrossed her arms and glanced at the inspection form, she spotted the tiniest shard of stainless steel peeking out at the top of her shirt.

Charlie smiled. "Clean bill of health," he said. "See ya 'round town!"

Phew!

Jan loped into the stockroom to grab a fresh set of whites and change into them in the adjoining bathroom/locker room.

Alma watched through the leaded glass windows as Charlie got back into his car. He caught her gaze and waved at her. When his taillights came on, she finally extricated the scrubber, popping the top button off her shirt in the process. The button skittered across the stainless steel counter and landed on the floor.

"Shit," she said.

Alma decided to rinse out the pot scrubber and run it through the dish machine. That would probably sanitize it enough after its ride in her bra, she figured. Good illegal wire pot scrubbers weren't super-easy to come by.

Jessie exploded into laughter. "Oh, nice. *Very* nice," she said. "You had that gross thing down your shirt the whole time! Wow, check out the fish heads. They're huge. This one looks like Walter Cronkite. You know, CBS news?"

Jan walked back into the room tying a blue bandana around his head, and Jessie put her hand inside the fish head as if it were a puppet. "Hey, Jan! Check it *out!*" she said, and dropped her voice to a fake baritone. "And here, now, the news."

"What?" Jan looked a little puzzled, but then he laughed.

Jessie turned red, and threw the grouper head into a big stock pot on the stove.

"I said that because that fish looked just like *Walter Cronkite* the news guy. It totally did! Didn't you think so?" Jan and Jessie were laughing together over by the stove, now.

Alma felt just a little jealous.

That's ridiculous, she told herself, pulling down her copy of *The Moosewood Cookbook* from the shelf and turning to the page where she'd multiplied the cornbread recipe up to make enough for seventy-five people. "Good of you to pull the double shift, Jess," she said. "Mary told me she'll come in for you tomorrow if you want a long weekend. I'll call her and set it up if you want."

"Cool," said Jessie.

"I absolutely could have done tonight solo," said Jan. "But it's good I don't have to. All praise and thanks to the boss lady."

Alma caught herself staring at his chin. As usual, he hadn't shaved. His beard would be a reddish brown, darker than his hair. *He'd probably look fabulous with a beard instead of that stubble.* But wasn't stubble supposed to be sexy? *The boss lady? I don't think I like being called that.*

"Know what, Jan?" said Jessie. *"I* wouldn't do dinner by myself. *I* wouldn't want to close up this place alone. After second dinner when there's no one in the offices upstairs and the dining halls are empty, this building gets super, super creepy. Breakfast shift can be pretty weird in the wintertime, too, like before dawn. I don't like to be alone here when it's dark."

Alma had heard lots of talk like that since she'd taken the Bright Day job. One of the first things anyone told her was to keep at least two staff members in the Main at night. Everyone agreed the place was haunted, but nobody seemed to know any more details than that. You *absolutely* weren't supposed to talk to the kids about it. People working alone in the building tended to get freaked out—and leave their posts. Something her mom would've loved to death. *If she knew—but I'm not going to tell her.*

Alma's mom claimed to be psychic. "I can always tell when people we know are going to die," she liked to brag. "I have a vision of their faces right before I go to sleep, glowing and surrounded by a greater darkness." A *greater darkness*. That had scared the snot out of Alma as a child. Now, she tried to maintain a healthy skepticism about such things. But she'd gotten stuck by herself in the Bright Day kitchen at night a few times. It was weird how you felt watched when no one was there.

New job, though, so she couldn't run screaming to her car because it felt like someone was looking over her shoulder as she figured out what spices to order, or reorganized the pasta and canned tomatoes. There was rent to pay. The divorce had left Alma with little in the bank. She was just getting caught up now. Every time she'd thought it was almost settled, Stefan's lawyer had found something else to fight over. There had even been a certified letter over two record albums and a cast-iron frying pan.

"Hey, I caught something out the corner of my eye the other night, when Mary and I were locking up," said Jan. "I thought it was a kid, so I went back into the riverside dining hall to make sure we weren't shutting anyone in. The room was empty, but the tea urn was back on and I *swear* I'd pulled the plug."

"Whoa," said Jessie. "*Cah-reepy*. How many onions you want chopped?"

"Eight of the really big Spanish ones. Coarse chop, with a knife. Don't put them in the CuisinArt—makes 'em mushy. I'll do the potatoes myself."

Jessie nodded and drew a chef's knife back and forth across the sharpening steel. "You are *totally* walking me to my car tonight, Jan,"

"Be glad to. Consider yourself protected from all ghosts and goblins."

Alma measured corn meal and gave herself full permission to envy her prep cook.

While the corn bread was baking, Alma got on the phone and arranged for Mary to come in the next day. Then, she changed back into her jeans and tucked her steel-toed work boots into her locker. She slipped into her fuzzy turquoise jacket and walked into the kitchen to say goodnight. Jessie skipped over to hug her.

"I'm so glad you got Max's old job, Al," she said. "It's *fun* working here, now. And I actually love that coat. I'm sorry I said it looked like a bathroom rug this morning."

Al. My name is Alma. Al-ma.

"Thanks," she said. "It *does* look like a bathroom rug. That's why I bought it. Have a party, you two. G'night!" She beamed at Jan.

"Night, boss!" he said, without looking up.

Oh, well. Aced the Health Department. Could have been a worse day. She slid into her beloved dusty red 1966 Valiant, and drove toward the school's big wrought iron gate in the gathering twilight. As she made the turn onto Route 9W, she glanced back at the main building. Someone in a corner room on the third floor was flashing the lights on and off repeatedly.

Ghosts! Nah. Probably just one of the kids slipped away from his residence group, screwing around, being ... inappropriate.

Chapter Two

Alma lived on the second floor of a Victorian house that must have belonged to someone important back in the day. Not anyone important as whoever built Bright Day's buildings in the 20s, but someone who'd had money enough for a big place with tall ceilings and marble fireplaces. These days, the place had uneven floors, uncertain gutters, and questionable electrical wiring. And it was drafty. The pretty violet and green stained glass at the top of Alma's living room windows rattled in the wind.

But there were hardwood floors that went perfectly with her thrift shop Turkish rugs. She'd inherited a green velvet old lady couch and reading chair from her grandparents. Her ex had hated them, but she'd always loved them, and now they finally had a home. So what if they ate up her living room? You could flop on them with a book.

Alma hung her coat on the wobbly coat tree she'd found on the street and headed straight for the shower to wash off a day in the kitchen. Taking a shower at her apartment was a little complicated. The bathroom had a claw-foot tub with a curtain you had to fasten just so. She was determined never to flood *her* bathroom, though— the last night of her marriage was something she'd never be able to unsee.

After she was no longer a Szchuan orange chicken bomb, Alma ran a soapy cloth over the bathroom mirror to clear it, and took a wide-toothed comb to her wild mop of blonde hair. Her kinky curls had made her an impressive hippie chick in the 70s, back when she'd almost been able to sit on them. She'd cut the long length to her shoulders on a whim a few months before she took the Bright Day job. She liked her hair that way now, just wild enough, and easy to get under a toque or a scarf for work. She dried off and dressed before walking barefoot into her own kitchen.

Alma's fridge was almost empty. All there was were eggs, a carton of Tropicana OJ, a big bottle of North Mountain Chablis, and because she was a chef, after all, some prosciutto and a hunk of good parmesan cheese. Like many food professionals she knew, Alma didn't cook much at home—unless, of course, she had a heavy date to impress. But she almost never had heavy dates. Cooking all day made you *tired.* Besides getting a divorce... Well, that made you tired, too. *And* cautious.

Thursday night. She ran over Friday's breakfast and lunch menu in her head. Bagels, scrambled eggs, sausages... All the stuff for the tacos was ordered, there were even ripe avocados and— Oh, dinner! Right, she *had* called the Hudson Market for those pork chops. Mike would deliver those tomorrow, along with Saturday's London broils.

Stop it! Stop thinking about work, she told herself. That was hard to do. A month or so of paychecks was the only thing between Alma and her parents' crazy household down in Briarcliff Manor. Or sharing an apartment with a bunch of her fellow kitchen rats—that is to say, an apartment full of hangovers, aspirin, and beat-up looking, transparent-skinned guys who deeply enjoyed cocaine. Never again!

Alma got herself a glass of wine. North Mountain Chablis was hardly a vintage delight. The best thing about it was the price. But it was way better than the vile stuff from her last job.

She walked into her living room, still trying not to think about cooking. Too bad the only way she could do that was to try not to think about Jan—and fail.

Why am I so hung up on him tonight? Okay, maybe he's not so bad. Even though he is a total kitchen rat. Jan's other job was tending bar on the weekends at The Very Last Old Fashioned Saloon, which was a dumb name for anything. Locals called it The Old Fascist. Nobody under fifty drank there. It was rumored to be owned by an Italian who'd been on the wrong side of things in World War II. Alma imagined Jan in the dark green vest and tie the Old Fascist bar staff all had to wear, along with a long white apron tied at the waist. He probably looked great.

But Jan didn't act like a coke head. He looked healthy enough. *Maybe I should go down to The Old Fascist one night, have a couple of glasses of wine.* She thought about Jan standing behind The Old Fascist's long mahogany bar, with its dim lights and engraved mirrors and been-there-forever murals of peacocks and morning glories. Old man joint or not, the room was kind of beautiful. She thought of Jan pouring her a glass of wine … or no. Maybe she'd ask for a real cocktail. That would be glamorous. He'd use a silver shaker and strain it into a long-stemmed glass.

He'd lean over the bar, then. *Glad you came in*, he'd say to her, and the last of the rumpled, wrinkle-faced crew that usually populated the place would quietly begin shuffling out the door.

It's almost time to close, he'd say. *Don't you hurry, though...* He'd pour himself a drink, too, sit down beside her…and then… Alma felt her breath quicken.

No.

No, no, no.

He works for me, for God's sake. I can't be fantasizing about someone who works for me. That's... The word "inappropriate" occurred to her. But how long had it been?

The truth? Ever since she'd left Stefan. Two years. Yeah, there had been several almost-happeneds. And there was a bona fide, good faith attempt at The Dread Deed with Sid, chef at The Blue Peppermill, a place with great river views and indifferent food. Alma had gone out and hit the bars with the other kitchen rats one Sunday night when she was still at Alberto's. She'd gotten into a big conversation about poetry (of all things!) with Sid. He actually knew who Elizabeth Bishop was. He'd quoted Emily Dickinson! And he laughed easily. Sid was tall and wiry, with warm brown eyes...

But he drank even harder than Alma's ex, and the truth about guys that drank that much involved lots of moaning, groaning and crashing around in the sheets— and then, almost always, a highly untimely collapse. When Sid actually fell asleep in the middle of everything, Alma was sweaty, sore ... and frustrated.

He didn't call her back after that—a relief, really—and probably the only real relief available from Sid. He'd ended up moving to Thermopolis, Wyoming. Alma had found that out when he sent her a postcard of a group of tourists enjoying the hot springs there. Plenty of easy work, he said, at the Holiday Inn's steak house. He was running the joint now. She should come out, grab a gig.

Yeah, *right*.

Alma put her wine down and searched through her record albums for Respighi's *Pines of Rome*. She'd had been a rock and roller for most of her life, but the classical stuff had also been easy on her ears lately. *Pines of Rome* was her favorite cool-out album side, especially the movement that was supposed to describe the trees near Rome's ancient catacombs.

There. Alma put the LP on her turntable and had

another sip of wine. She curled up on her grandma's couch and opened her copy of Mary Stewart's *The Last Enchantment*. She'd been loving that book. But tonight, she was too restless to let it carry her back to the days of Merlin and King Arthur.

Six-twenty. Full darkness outside now. Alma closed the book, and stood at her living room window. She looked down the hill toward downtown Engelhook. There were too many leaves still on the trees for her to see the Hudson River yet, but lights from downtown were just beginning to twinkle through a few bare branches when the wind blew. They would be just about to serve second dinner at Bright Day. An image of Jan in his blue bandana snuck into Alma's brain and she quashed it.

Second dinner. She wasn't hungry. Cooks tasted stuff all day, and Alma often had to remind herself to eat a real meal when she got home. It was easier to go out, but not on nights before she had to get up at 5:30 to open the kitchen for breakfast the next morning. She decided to make herself some eggs, and turned up the stereo a bit so she could hear it in the kitchen.

Alma was in the middle of folding a nicely golden parmesan and prosciutto omelet onto a plate when she began to sense something that almost wasn't there.

And then it *was* there. A draft? What had just made the lights blink? Alma glanced up at the circa 1940 glass light fixture on her kitchen ceiling with its on/off pull chain. *Bad wiring*, she thought. *Gotta be.*

But there it was again—that almost breeze. The pull chain swung back and forth just a little bit.

Wait. Was that someone's *breath* on her neck?

Alma's stomach went cold. She dropped the pan and it clattered onto the burner. *Shit, I locked the door, didn't I?* Engelhook didn't have much of a crime rate.

There had been some break-ins over the summer. But weren't those all on the other end of town, where the rich folks lived? Who'd even bother to break into Alma's building? Who'd have been able to get past her snoopy landlord, who lived downstairs with his mom?

Except there it was a third time—a puff of something, almost imperceptible, chilly and moist. Then, a smell like wet earth. And then … a presence. It felt like someone was watching her plate her dinner—very closely. Someone was leaning over her shoulder! It felt an awful lot like being in the Main at Bright Day, alone.

What the hell?

"Mind the fire," said a man's voice. It wasn't a deep voice. It was almost high-pitched, gentle.

Alma gasped and spun around.

Right beside her, surrounded by what her mother would have called a "circle of greater darkness" stood a pale-faced man about her own height, with shoulder-length dark brown hair pulled neatly back into a queue. His clothes didn't look like anything Alma had seen outside of an art museum. A long, black jacket with many buttons worn over a loose-fitting ivory-colored shirt.

Despite the blackness around him, the man seemed … bright. As if he held light inside him somehow. Alma flashed back to one of her mother's favorite spooky dinner party stories.

"Even though she was in *Chicago* at the time and I was *here,* I swear I saw Aunt Louise's face *glowing*—in a *circle of greater darkness*…" she'd said. "And her heart stopped beating that very night."

The man standing next to Alma touched her shoulder. His fingertips were either very hot or very cold.

"The *fire*," he said. "Mind the *fire!*"

"The fire?" Alma looked down. "Oh," she said,

and turned off the burner on her stove.

The ring of darkness around him vanished. The man nodded and then smiled. "Your omelet smells delicious," he said. It was weird because now Alma wasn't frightened—just breathless from having been so startled.

A ghost. Of *course* he was a ghost—even though before that night, she'd never felt anything spooky at her place in the almost-year she'd lived in it. Alma still had the plate with the omelet on it in one hand. Ghosts didn't *eat*, did they? She held it out to him anyway.

"Go ahead and have your supper," he said. "I don't need food. I take it you understand why."

Alma nodded, not sure what to say. For a ghost, the man looked rather … dashing, she decided was the world. He must have been muscular in life. There were nicely rounded biceps under that loose shirt, and they showed when he moved his arms. His knee knickers fit tightly over a flat belly, and his stockings made his calves look like they were made out of smooth, white marble. His eyes were a startling, luminous golden brown.

"Sadly, we are still perfectly able to smell a good meal cooking."

"We?" Alma said.

The man nodded. "Your dead," he said, solemnly.

"*My* dead?" she said.

"Well, you *live* here, don't you? So, I'm *your* dead, now." He stopped looking so serious then and as if guys in knee knickers and white stockings were born doing it, he opened her refrigerator and pulled out the bottle of Chablis. "Here, give me your glass," he said, and topped it off. The glow from the refrigerator's light made him even more luminous—and just the slightest bit translucent.

"Thanks," she said, although it was *her* wine. She put her plate and glass down on a little enamel-topped kitchen table she'd bought at a local church thrift shop and pulled out one of the table's funky old chairs for herself.

"Fork? Napkin?" he said, pulling those things out of the drawers next to Alma's stove. Alma used cloth napkins from the restaurant supplier—big white ones.

"You know where my things are," she said, spreading the napkin across her lap.

"That shouldn't surprise you," he said. "Eat your omelet while it's hot. Go ahead."

Alma took a bite. "Um, the pepper grinder on the stove?" she said. "Could you, please?"

"My lady." He smiled and handed it to her with a little bow.

She ground a little pepper over her plate and took another bite and sipped her wine. He sat down across from her, put his elbows on the table, and his chin in his hands.

"I enjoy watching you eat."

"Okay, I guess. It's not … weird?"

"No."

A ghost is watching me eat an omelet. "What's your name?"

"Bartholomew Addison Jenkins," he said. "These days, I just use Bart."

"These days. But you've been here since you…"

"Since 1784," he said.

"Which was when you died, I guess."

"I must tell you, dear lady, saying that to one of us is considered rude. In better ghostly circles, that is. Some of us are not aware we are dead. Some of us do not like to be reminded of it."

"But you called yourself *my* dead…"

Bart threw his head back and laughed. "No, no, no. *I'm* not sensitive about it. Geoff Brussy is, though, terribly but he always was a hothead. I swear he acted as if he was ignorant of his own passing for at least a century. Forgive me, Alma. Finish your supper."

"But you know *my* name. Oh. Because you live here. So I guess you see and hear…" *Everything. He'd have seen me do everything I've ever done in this apartment…*

"I try not to spy," Bart said. "And I'm often asleep. Daytimes almost always. Some evenings, too. Ghosts are capable of sleeping for years. Depending on what we've been up to, of course. We're made of energy and sometimes, our energy … just *dissipates*. So our acquaintances tend to … vanish. It's quite upsetting. I've lost a number of friends that way. Other ghosts, I mean. Dissipation is hard on our … um, relationships."

"Your *relationships*?" said Alma.

"Isn't that what you call it, these days? Or do you still say 'having lovers?' People said that for quite a while. You'll forgive me. I slept through half of the nineteen sixties. The residents of this apartment in the 70s were—what do you call it again? Pot heads. Boring."

"Ghosts have … *relationships*?" Alma remembered her metaphysical poetry class from New Paltz. "The grave's a fine and private place, but none, I think, do there embrace," she said.

"Oops. Guess I mentioned death again. I'm sorry. I didn't mean to…"

Bart chuckled. "Oh, that's fine. Andrew Marvel. Good. Very good. 'To His Coy Mistress.' He was utterly wrong, of course. About embracing. Of course, it's a bit … challenging for us, but hardly *impossible*."

Alma shook her head. She'd finished her omelet, and put her plate in the sink.

"Please," said Bart. "I've been wanting to talk to you for months and months. Why don't you finish your wine in the living room? I'll turn over the record. I've been enjoying the music. Both sides of that album are really very good. I like 'The Fountains of Rome' too. We couldn't have imagined Respighi during my days in the flesh."

"You'll *turn over the record*. Oh, because you…"

"I *do* like to keep up. Who poured you wine from the … refrigerator? Although, I don't understand why people of your age prefer it so icy."

Alma followed Bart into the living room, still wondering why things didn't seem odder than they were. She remembered the Casper the Friendly Ghost cartoons she'd seen as a little girl. This ghost was acting—well, perhaps a bit more flirty than friendly. He only glowed a bit as they walked through the dim hallway that connected her rooms. *You can hardly even tell he's translucent.* What had he seen of *her*, though? She was glad her frustrating night with Sid had been at his place.

As Bart bent over the turntable and flipped the record, the reading lamp by her couch highlighted the silver buttons of his coat. She curled up on the couch and put her wine glass on the glass-covered orange crate she'd turned into a coffee table.

Bart sat beside her, suspiciously close. He put an arm over the back of the couch, and Alma shook her head again. *That's the old sneaky-arm trick—like a high school kid. It's kind of cute.* She pulled her legs up under herself, and they quietly listened to the music.

"You're right," she said after a few minutes. "'Fountains' is really good, too. I almost never listen to that side."

Bart made a quiet harrumphing noise.

Do ghosts clear their throats? Apparently so.

"Dear lady," he said. "Although I do try not to snoop, as you would say, I have indeed observed your solitude. Let me assure you, your life will soon be happier." He slid even closer to her.

Okay. Now the ghost is absolutely coming on to me. This is really happening. Oh, hell—why not? He's not bad—for a dead guy.

"Um, Bart?" she said. His eyes really were a startling color—almost bronze... "You can't actually be..."

Bart set his fingertips on her cheeks, looked into her eyes, and sighed. Then he smiled. "You think this is a ridiculous situation. It's *not* ridiculous," he said. "Not at all. Allow me to demonstrate ... with your permission, m'lady."

Somehow, that was funny, and Alma giggled. "Granted."

Bart's hands were impossibly soft and gentle— and his touch had some of the same fire-and-ice buzz that she'd felt before in the kitchen when he'd tried to get her attention. He guided her lips to his, and gave her what would have been a tiny peck—from anyone else. It shot a bolt of fire straight through her.

"*Oh*," she said. It took a minute to get her breath. "Wow. That was... Do ghosts usually have *relationships* with—I don't know how to say this without getting into it all again ... people who are still alive?"

"No, actually. In fact, I've never heard of it. Ever." His hands were in her hair now, and urgent.

Her scalp tingled from his stroking. Were his fingers hot or really cold?

"I'd forgotten," he said, "about this. All of this— the warmth and sweetness of the living. Ah, Alma, your lovely, lovely hair." Bart sighed.

Alma closed her eyes, and felt his hands slide to

her shoulder blades and slip down her back. Was she trembling or shivering? His lips were on hers again. She opened her mouth to his—and felt like she had been caught in a shower of sparks. His tongue was so cool… The lights in her apartment flickered twice and then went out. And Bart vanished.

Chapter Three

Alma had a flashlight in the bedroom but of course it didn't work. *Could have sworn I just put new batteries in this thing.* After dropping it back into the chest of drawers beside her bed, she felt around until she found matches to light the three candles in Mason jars on the dresser in front of her mirror. They cast a little light, enough to see that her hair now looked like seventh grade science class—the day the girls had taken turns getting hooked to a Van de Graaf generator. She tried to smooth standing-on-end strands down and they crackled with static.

"*Bart*?" she called. No answer.

There was a loud knock on her door, and her landlord's odd, scratchy voice. "Alma, Alma! You okay?" It was good having Peter Koslov and his mother living in the building because he fixed things—well, sort of—and bad as the two of them really *did* snoop. But if he liked you, Peter left kielbasa in your refrigerator sometimes. Which was totally weird, totally sweet … and just a little stalky. It was tasty kielbasa though, so there was that. He'd gifted Alma with several packages.

"Alma!" he called again.

"I'm fine, Peter." She picked up one of the candles and walked to the door. Peter was in his late forties, never married. His short, slicked-back hair looked like it had been grey the day he was born.

"Good, good," he said. "I go 'em to basement, fix 'em up." Alma could never quite place where his accent came from. He and his mom owned quite a few other cool but dilapidated buildings in town, and there were lots of theories about where he came from. *My money's on Russia*. But he also sounded a bit like Tonto from the old Lone Ranger TV show. And wasn't kielbasa Polish?

"Thanks," she said. "I wasn't using the hair dryer or microwave."

"This is old building," said Peter. "Build 'em up in 1879. *Strong*, though. Very strong."

"I understand," said Alma, although she didn't quite.

Peter headed for the stairwell.

Alma closed the door, and walked through her apartment, looking for any sign of Bart. He couldn't have just *dissipated* because he tried to get frisky with the living? *The living,* thought Alma. It felt a little like being at a funeral thinking of herself that way.

The lights came back on and her turntable started back up with a groan. The wiring in her building was indeed pretty bad—she wasn't even allowed an air conditioner—but she'd only been using a couple of lights and her stereo. Then she remembered what Bart had said about ghosts being "made of energy." Was *he* what had drained her flashlight batteries? *Did I just manage to pop a circuit breaker by kissing a ghost*? Alma walked into her bedroom to blow out the candles and felt twenty times as restless as she had before Bart showed up.

She finally put MTV on the set by her bed. They were playing a Thomas Dolby video *Airwaves.* Even though its images were dark and moody, the flicker of cable TV seemed cheery and very much of the modern world. That was soothing. The night was chilly, the first time that fall she'd really wanted to put on a flannel nightgown. Alma climbed into the big old sleigh bed she'd painted bright yellow when she first moved to Englehook, and watched Kid Creole and the Coconuts, Toto, and Prince videos until she settled down enough to feel a little sleepy.

If Bart dissolved for keeps because he was doing

something he shouldn't have been, it would be kind of too bad. I've never felt anything like that in my whole life. Alma curled up on her side, clicked off the remote, and closed her eyes. Finally, her tired muscles won out over her prickly nerves and she fell asleep.

Morning came too soon, as it always did when she had to open up the kitchen to cook breakfast. The sky over the Hudson was just beginning to go pink as Alma parked her car outside the at Bright Day. There was a fine coating of frost on the school's softball field, and barely enough light for her to see that the maples near the parking circle had gone brilliantly golden. The kids were all asleep, but two overnight duty workers sat outside Sundog Cottage, smoking cigarettes and laughing. All the Bright Day residence buildings had names—Sundog, Eclipse, Saturn, Shooting Star.

Alma waved at them, and headed to the back door of the main building.

"Oh, *shit*." Either there was a new and supremely stupid person delivering for Catskill Bakery, or some kids had gotten loose the night before. The giant cardboard box containing her bread order—seven dozen bagels and a few Pullman loaves of whole wheat—had been used to prop open the building's back door. The flaps on the top of the carton were still folded over each other, but they looked dinged-up. That could mean only one thing. Alma kicked the box and it rocked back and forth. Something growled and scratched inside of it.

"Shit, shit, shit," she said, and kicked the box again. Two raccoons—one of them bigger than most Thanksgiving turkeys and very fat—exploded through the top of it and ran for the bushes. She kicked the box a third time, but nothing happened. There wasn't much in the way of bagels or bread left inside, and certainly nothing anyone with a working brain would feed to human beings after raccoons had been rolling around in it.

"Goddamn it," she said, and dragged the mauled bread order into the hall that led to the kitchen door.

"Taking the Lord's name *in vain!* I'm shocked, but maybe I shouldn't be."

Alma smelled pipe smoke.

There, leaning against the door to the kitchen was a man in knee britches and a loose white shirt like the one that Bart had worn—and, well … you could even say he glowed. As did the bowl of the pipe he was smoking, with a sort of yellowish green light. His salt and pepper was hair pulled into the same queue Bart wore. "*Good* morning, Alma," he said, smiling.

This time, Alma didn't even jump. *Oh, fabulous. Great. Another ghost. I guess I should be shocked I'm not shocked. You'd think he'd have at least scared off the damn raccoons. So what do I say to this one?* She stuck her hands in her pockets and put on her angriest boss-lady face. "Excuse me, Mister Whoever-You-Are, but I have to—"

The ghost with the pipe didn't let Alma finish her sentence. "Geoff Brussy. Miller, Patriot, and oldest resident of this fine establishment. And quite an improvement over what used to stand here it is, too. I imagine you'll be baking muffins to make up for the loss of your bread." He giggled. "Applesauce muffins. I hear yours are quite delicious! I've observed—"

"Oh, for the love of fuck. Tell me you watched me make them last week, when the same goddamn thing happened."

"Oh, *my!*" said Geoff, and tittered. "Bartholomew has got himself a spicy one, the dandy prat! I'll be confounded! I could have sworn the fool didn't even know he was dead!"

Alma felt her cheeks going red. "That's what he said about *you*. And Bart hasn't 'got himself' anyone!"

"Oh, it's 'Bart' is it? You say he *hasn't*? Then why does my lady blush? But I shouldn't keep you from your labor. I do enjoy the scent of hot applesauce muffins. Perhaps that's why I pushed your bread order outside and extended a kind bit of charity to the raccoons."

"You did *what*? Oh, for fuck's sake! Would you *just* get out of here? I mean vanish, get lost … *dissipate!*"

"Oh, my *goodness,*" said Geoff. "And with a temper!"

Then there was another voice, right behind her. Benny the Beemer, reporting for table setting and cleanup duty. "Alma, who are you talking to?"

Alma spun around. Benny was twelve. He was wearing his favorite blue and white "Money Helps" t-shirt with its picture of a lifesaver and a boat. As usual, his longish blond hair was tied back in a ponytail, to keep it out of the way in the kitchen. *There are way too many guys in ponytails around lately.*

"I wasn't talking to anyone," said Alma. "Only muttering to myself, I guess." It was hard to resist the temptation to glance over her shoulder, but if Geoff was still there, Benny wasn't giving any sign of having seen him.

"You said the *F-word*," said Benny. "Twice. You said the F-word and you were talking to yourself. That's *inappropriate.*"

"Yes," said Alma, "It *was* inappropriate. Very. I'm sorry, Benny. Would you like some applesauce muffins for breakfast? And scrambled eggs and sausages?"

"That would feel really good…" said Benny, "…in my *carburetor!*" He smiled a broad, closed-mouth smile. *"Ba-room! Brroom!"*

She wasn't really supposed to let him do that, but she didn't feel like she had the right to say much under the current circumstances. "Um, Benny, go wash your hands and get on a clean apron. Forks, knives and spoons on the tables. Juice glasses and napkins, okay? You want to mix up the OJ?"

"Oh-*kay*!" said Benny. Alma heard him switching to third gear as he ran into the kitchen—right past Geoff, whom she was now sure he couldn't see.

Geoff raised a hand, wriggled his greenish fingers in farewell, winked, and vanished into the dawn.

Chapter Four

It had been good cooking lunch with Mary. Her art was getting around in the local galleries, she'd just done a series of paintings on women and work. Cheerful, matter-of-fact portraits of architects and bankers and doctors. It was fun talking about that. Mary was so like her pictures, upbeat and honest. Plus she could really cook! Alma often wished she worked with her middays, instead of Jessie. But it was also good having someone as solid as Mary at Bright Day when Alma wasn't there. Because of her, Alma had forgotten about the reason she'd had to bake applesauce muffins that morning. *Almost* forgotten, that was.

"You should hang with me and Cleo more often, seriously," Mary was saying to her, as they finished cleanup. Cleo was Mary's long-time partner, a Bright Day social worker who collected African art. They had a top-floor apartment in the cool old brick building next to The Old Fascist downtown. Their place was full of Cleo's carvings and Mary's canvases—and it had a great view of the river. "I hardly see you anymore outside of work. I'd like to do a painting of *you* one of these days. Maybe not one of the women-and-work ones, though. I really like the look of you with your hair out of that chef's hat."

"Yeah. We really should get together more." Alma thought of Bart then, how he'd liked her hair, too. She couldn't help it, she shivered a little. "You want to take home this leftover taco stuff? Looks like there's plenty for two in there. You could freeze it for some night you come home tired and hungry."

"Thanks," said Mary. "Think I will. Those were great. Ground coriander, huh? I'd have just gone with cumin and chili powder. And lots of garlic, of course."

"Yeah, I like the coriander lately. Here, let me get that." Alma picked up the big, square pot she'd been using to sauté everything lately. It had worked nicely for the taco meat.

"You're the *boss!* I don't know why you wash your own pots."

"Oh, c'mon, Mary. That's just silly. Hudson Market will be here in like two minutes. Check in the order if you want work to do and then go have a sit down for a bit. You're on for dinner, too. Pace yourself." Alma carried the pot over to the sink.

"Well, all right, then. If you insist." Mary rummaged in the shoebox full of cassette tapes next to the kitchen boom box and pulled out *Labor of Lust* by Nick Lowe. "So, pork chops tonight and I have Jo Beth to prep? She's such an outstanding cook. We'll be done by 7:30 easy. Let's get you out of the house for a change. Come down to our apartment around eight, and we'll go bother Jan at his bar gig. It'll be fun." The opening guitar chords to *Cruel to be Kind* bounced off the white-tiled kitchen walls. Mary untied her apron, shook it out, and retied it around her almost nonexistent hips.

Jan at his bar gig. Alma ran water into the pan and once more paged through her mental photo album of Very Cute Jan. His stubbly chin and blue bandana. *Hmmm. Jan in that long Old Fashioned Saloon apron, dark green vest and tie.* She reran her very pleasant fantasy of him shaking up a cocktail for her, wiry arms over his head as he held the silver and glass shaker.

But then Alma thought about kissing *Bart!* That had felt... Well, really pretty darn great, to be honest.

She started thinking about Geoff, too. It was a cool, sunny, late October afternoon. Near Halloween, sure—but nothing felt haunted at that moment. Unless, of course, you were the type of woman with a taste for kissing ghosts. Maybe having a little chat with their old friends on her way into work... *That son of a bitch ghost put my bread order outside to get trashed*, thought Alma, scrubbing taco scorch out of the side of the pan.

"Hel-looo! Earth to Alma!" said Mary and Alma slopped a wave of soap and hot water out of the sink and onto her apron.

"Oh, shit," she said. "Okay. Sure, let's go bug Jan tonight. I'm totally up for it."

"Do you think he's cute? Jessie thinks he's just adorable, you know."

"Did she *say* that?"

"No, but anyone can tell," said Mary. "Look at you. You're sopping wet. Told ya, you should have let me do that pot."

The dishwater that had soaked Alma went from warm to uncomfortably chilly very fast. She untied her apron, and peeled it away from her stomach. "You think Jessie's after Jan?"

"Nah. She's just a flirt. You can think someone is adorable without wanting to act on it," said Mary. "Hey, *you're* pretty adorable, but you're straight as the day is long. Besides, I have the best damn girlfriend on the whole planet. There's cute and there's putting-the-moves-on cute."

"This is true," said Alma.

Then the kitchen door opened, and the delivery man from Hudson Market walked in with the London broil and broccoli for Saturday night dinner, along with a few more crates of local apples and a big bag of potatoes. Alma made a beeline toward the delivery.

"Hey, hey, hey!" said Mary. "Cut that stuff out. You said you were going to let *me* check in the order. I'll make sure everything's okay. This is the voice of reason talking, Alma. You are going to burn yourself right out. Get your paperwork done and go home. Now! This kitchen is running fine, and you're going out tonight for a change!"

Well, then. Guess I am, then.

After Alma changed back into her street clothes and put on her bathroom-rug-jacket, Mary and Jo Beth were already hard at work prepping the macaroni and cheese that was going to go along with the chops. Mary had a white sauce going, and Jo Beth was already cutting up chunks of cheddar for the grater.

Those two really do work at the speed of light. Mary is right. Things are going fine here. I need to relax. A Friday night out will do me good. Alma had almost forgotten she didn't have to come in the next day. She headed for her car.

The phone was ringing when she opened the door to her apartment. Alma hustled inside to grab the call and then she sighed. It was her mother.

Bet anything Mom's got a bomb to drop. That's the only reason she ever calls.

"I'm just fine," she said, "How are you, Mom?"

Philomena was a woman who purred into telephones, and she was in full feline mode. "Terr-ific," she said. "But you know, my dear, I've been just little concerned about you, lately. I mean with the divorce final and everything. Such a *blow!"*

"It's not a blow! I told you, I'm fine. You know I love my job. I—"

"Ugh! That job of yours! And poor old Stefan. You know the divorce has been *very* hard on Stefan. He seems rather … distraught! Your father and I had dinner with him the other night and I'm afraid he got a little tipsy—"

"Stefan *always* gets a little tipsy," said Alma. She

pulled the phone cord over to the couch and sat down. "He gets more than a little tipsy practically daily."

"Your father and I think he *misses* you."

"That's fine," said Alma. "In fact, that's the plan. He can miss me for keeps. So why does this make you concerned about *me?*"

"Oh, you'll think your old mother is being silly, Alma."

"Probably. Tell me anyway."

"Oh, *Alma!* I saw your face last night—*in a circle of greater darkness!*"

Alma instantly felt nauseous. *Oh, No. Bart.* "So you called me up to say that you think I'm going to *die?* Isn't that what all those stories you used to tell were about—this great-auntie and that old uncle who showed up in your dark circle and promptly dropped dead?"

"No, no, no! I don't think that you're going to *die*, honey. I—"

"But that's what always happens, isn't it? You see the face and bam—dead." *Maybe I should be frightened.* And now she was. But mostly she was furious with her mother.

"Oh, Alma, I was *exaggerating!* Heavens. You should understand that. It was just dinner table conversation. You know, to keep things lively. I didn't really have *premonitions of death!*"

"*What?* All those glow in the dark stories weren't true? You were *lying?*"

"Well, technically speaking."

"So you never actually saw *any* of that stuff? You just said that you did? Really?"

"That's the thing. I used to have… Well, *feelings*, I'd call them. But I never actually had a real vision *until last night!* Alma, just before I was going to sleep, I *did* see you. Your face, lit brightly against the shadows! It was exactly like in my stories. I mean, exactly like them, if I hadn't made them all up."

"Oh." Alma's head swum. *My mom is the kind of crazy that makes other people every bit as crazy as she is.* She looked out her window and wrapped the phone's cord around her fingers. The afternoon light was beginning to fade a bit, but the low sun caught a Japanese maple by her building's driveway and lit it up like a flame.

"I do hope I didn't upset you. But I wanted you to be *careful*, you know."

"Um, thanks, Mom. I guess."

"So you will be—careful, I mean?"

"I will be."

"Oh, good! Do you have some *wonderful* plans for tonight?"

"Going out with some friends."

"And you'll think a little about poor old Stefan, all alone in the world?"

"I do not believe that poor old Stefan is all alone in the world," said Alma.

She got off the phone and carried her shopping bag to the kitchen. Fresh milk for her morning coffee, good coffee beans for her grinder, a loaf of whole wheat bread from the new bakery in town. Alma stowed the groceries and then walked slowly through her apartment, peering into all the corners.

"*Bart?*" she called. "You around?"

Silence. Nothing. The beginnings of sunset outside.

Alma wanted to ask Bart about the circle of darkness. He *had* appeared to her in one. There was also the matter of timing. The night before—and that intense kiss! Was *that* why her mother had seen what she did? That is, if Philomena was telling the truth *this* time—but even if she was actually lying about having lied—a feat only she could pull off—it was a pretty creepy piece of business.

She considered Bart's kiss once again and felt the sharp string of remembered electricity. *That is what's really nuts,* thought Alma. *It's as detached from reality as any of the kids down at Bright Day. Mary's right. I have absolutely got to get out more.* She summoned up a stubble-cheeked, blue bandannaed image of Jan again. *There. That was much better.* Time for a shower and a night downtown.

Chapter Five

Alma was wearing her favorite bar-crawl outfit. It was her favorite because it wasn't blatantly sexy. A not-too-tight dark red sweater that went down almost to her knees and a pair of black leggings with stirrups that held them tightly inside her matching lace-up booties. The sweater draped and hugged her in all the right places, and its V-neck let a strap of the only black lace bra Alma owned peek out. She'd taken the trouble to blow dry her hair into an impressive blonde nimbus around her head, get her eyeliner on evenly, and to streak just a tiny bit of blue glitter gel in her hair over her right eyebrow.

Mary and Cleo sat next to her in matching grey sleeveless t-shirts despite the cool October night, denim jackets draped over the back of their bar stools. One of the stranger things about cooking for a living was that you seldom saw your coworkers' hair except away from work. Mary's was long and chestnut-colored with just a little wave in it. Her partner, Cleo, had an Afro cut short enough to be business-like with her young clients at Bright Day. She wore a pair of ivory-colored big star earrings. *Cleo always looks great.*

Cleo and Mary were trying to make Jan blush, and it wasn't exactly working.

But the comment Jan had just tossed back at Mary about wanting to walk in on the two of them 'just lapping up that exotic flavor you two ladies prefer' was… Well, there was teasing, and there was gross. That was *gross*. Seriously gross. Jan seemed delighted to have said it, too—as if actually putting something like that into words marked him as a sexy bad boy.

For God's sake, Cleo's dad was Korean, and her mom is Black. Exotic flavor, indeed. So it's racist and *disgusting besides. If Mary's not pissed off at him, I am*, thought Alma. *And the three of us have to work together in my kitchen!*

Cleo drained the last of her beer and rolled her eyes. Mary slipped her bare arms back into her jacket and snorted. "Yeah, yeah. I get it. Ha, ha, ha. You should be so lucky, big guy."

Jan grinned. He was clean-shaven tonight. Clean-shaven Jan was not, *such* a terrible thing to observe. But that comment. *Ick.*

Except then Cleo cracked up and Mary joined her in a belly laugh.

Really? They really thought that was okay? I thought they were getting ready to leave. Maybe not. Maybe I should just play along... Alma caught sight of herself in the mirror behind Jan's head. Her hair with its blue glitter was pretty impressive in the dim barroom. *I look pretty good. I came down here to have fun. Maybe I'm taking things too seriously again.* She peeked at Jan again. *So, Jan is a lunkhead. He's a very good-looking lunkhead. Maybe it was just a dumb joke.*

Okay. She would say something flirty. She drank the last of her second glass of wine first.

"Hey, Jan, you're all nice and smoothy-smooth tonight. Shaved off that bad boy stubble, did you?" *Oh, shit. That sounded totally stupid. Besides, I'm his boss. I can't be saying stuff like that.*

Jan reached over the bar, took her hand, and pulled it to his chin. Alma drew in her breath sharply, and tried to disguise it by laughing.

Mary snorted again.

"Wanna cop a feel?" His cheeks were baby-butt smooth, and fragrant with some sort of shaving product. "And another drink?"

"Um, *yes*," said Alma, suddenly and earnestly

enough that Cleo erupted into laughter again. "I want you to make me something … *glamorous*. I'm tired of wine."

Jan dropped Alma's hand. "An Aviation, then. Old Man Bucci just taught me this one. From Prohibition time. Hang on." He pulled two dusty bottles out from underneath the bar, grabbed a big bottle of Beefeater's Gin off the glass shelves behind him and dumped a bit of everything into a cocktail shaker with lemon juice and ice.

Then, it was exactly like Alma's fantasy. Jan shook the drink dramatically over his head and strained it into a long-stemmed cocktail glass. "Wait a minute," he said, and dangled a maraschino cherry on a stem in front of Alma's face before dramatically dropping it into the cocktail. "A *cherry*. But you only get *one!*"

Another stupid joke. Ugh, but oh well.

"That is what I've heard," Alma said, "about cherries." Jan handed the drink to her, raising one eyebrow. It was very pretty, opalescent and pale violet. The good-looking lunkhead had mixed her a very romantic-looking drink—and a delicious one. And, as she found out in a few minutes, a very, very powerful one. It probably had been a bad idea to have had whole wheat toast with peanut butter for dinner. But after a day in the kitchen, she hadn't been hungry and she'd been in a hurry to get the evening started. Cleo and Mary sipped the Heinekens Jan had slid across the bar in their direction. The conversation died for a few minutes.

"So, do you like it?" Jan asked Alma. His eyes were dark brown, and they were now focused sharply on her bra strap.

Alma nodded. "It's *amazing*," she said, sipped, and was out of words.

"What's in that thing, girl?" asked Cleo, after a few minutes. "Look at you *smiling*!"

Am I? Alma checked with the mirror again and saw herself grinning a big, loopy grin. Her lips were a little numb. She still had about half of her drink left.

"Um, Jan? Besides gin and lemon, what did you put in here?"

Jan got out the dusty bottles again. "Maraschino liqueur and…" He squinted at the smaller and dustier of the two. "Cah-rhem dee Violet. I don't speak French. You can't get the stuff anymore in the States. Bucci's got half a case downstairs and when it's gone, it's gone. I only make Aviations for *very special* customers. That one is on the house. For my one and only boss lady."

So lunkhead or not a lunkhead? Or is he just trying to get me really smashed? Jan turned his brightest smile on her, which really was pretty dazzling. *So what if I'm his boss lady? Maybe he's only being kind of… I don't know. Affectionate. That's cool.*

"*Hmmm…*" said Mary.

An order for four scotch and sodas and a Stinger came in from a bunch of grandfatherly men over at a table by the door. Alma watched Jan pour white crème de menthe and brandy into a cocktail shaker with ice. He did a little jig as he shook that drink, again holding the shaker over his head.

"You sure are one silly white boy," said Cleo.

Jan stuck his tongue out at her. The waitress who brought over the order had vanished, so he put the drinks on a tray and carried them over himself. Alma watched the way he moved through the shadowy bar. *Men say idiotic things sometimes*, she thought, and sipped a bit more of her drink. *He is pretty cute…*

A blast of cold air blew in from outside, along with the sound of Jessie DeCicco's belly laugh. She had on a black leather motorcycle jacket that was about five sizes too big for her and a pair of tight, acid-washed jeans. Her curly brown hair was pulled into a messy bun on one side of her head.

"Jan!" she yelled.

He took two long steps over to her and slapped her on the behind, hard enough that you could hear it all the way over by the bar. That caused raised eyebrows from the table of older gentlemen. Jessie winked at them and gave Jan a big, sloppy kiss. "God, I *love* this jacket! Thanks for letting me steal it last night!" she said. "Could I have another one of those Aviation things you make?"

Oh, thought Alma. *So that's how it is. Silly me to have worried about people not getting along in my kitchen. Those two seem to be doing just great.*

"*Hey*, Alma," said Mary, quietly. She turned her gaze from the Jessie-and-Jan floorshow and nodded. "I think it's time to drink up and mosey." She punched Cleo in the arm, gently. "C'mon, m'love."

Alma tipped back the rest of her Aviation and stumbled a little getting off the barstool.

"Steady as she goes," said Cleo, taking her arm.

Jessie skipped over as Jan bent over the scotch and soda table and said something that made the men there laugh. "You guys aren't *leaving*?"

Alma faked a smile. "I think I'm just a little tipsy," she said, and that was true. She wasn't dinner-party-with-the-ex drunk, but she would need a little time away from things like Aviations before she drove her car home.

"Oh, you're so cute with your sweater, though!" said Jessie.

Alma briefly considered decking her. *She's a decent prep, though. She is a very decent prep. Even though I wish I worked with Mary mornings.*

"See ya Monday, boss!" said Jan.

Boss.

"Let's us three get a pizza," said Mary. She gave Jessie a smile that was even a bit more fake than Alma's. "Do watch out for those Aviations, Jessie-child," she said. "I hear they're deadly."

Alma followed her and Cleo outside and upstairs to their apartment next door, where they ordered and made short work of a Garbage Pie from Arturo's. Arturo's delivered late and Garbage Pies had all the toppings you could ever think about putting on a pizza. Sausage, pepperoni, pepper, onions, mushrooms. They were just the thing for soaking up two glasses of wine and a blindingly strong cocktail.

Chapter Six

Alma wrapped her arms around herself as she walked to her car. The drinks had mostly worn off, and the night had turned quite cold. It had been stupid vanity not to wear a jacket. She slid behind the wheel and looked out her windshield at the river for a moment. This far north, the water was fairly dark at night. No New York City glow to reflect, just lights from the town of Hudson on the other side. There was a pretty little lighthouse and beyond it, on the opposite shore, the Hudson Correctional Facility, which was brightly lit. But there wasn't much else shining that late.

Alma thought about cranking up the heat in the Valiant and watching the river flow a bit more, but she was wiped out. Time to go home. It had been good hanging with Cleo and Mary. The Jan and Jess thing? That would just have to play itself out. *I didn't think Jan was quite that much of a jackass, but I seem to be the only one who got offended.* Ah, well… Just as well her mini-crush had run its course.

When she opened the door to her apartment, her stomach sank. A dim square of light flickered in the hall outside her bedroom door. *Yikes! Was I actually dumb enough to have left candles burning?* Alma was scolding herself for having been dangerously spacey when she realized that the light from her room did not come from any sort of flame.

It came from Bart. He was standing beside her bed in his high-collared, loose-fitting shirt and his knee britches. And that was … not really strange at all. Just the friendly, resident ghost. No danger of burning down the house. A relief—and Alma had to be honest with herself—a pleasant surprise.

"Good evening, m'lady," he said.

Alma opened her mouth to say hello back—and burped, instead. A Garbage Pie burp was an impressive burp. "Oh, wow. Excuse me."

Bart chuckled as she dropped her purse in the chair next to her dresser.

"Rich dinner?"

"A Garbage Pie," she said. "It sounds awful, but it's—you know what pizza pie is, right?"

"The previous residents of this apartment ate little else. I know well what Garbage Pies are," he said. "I do not fear them."

Then he stepped in front of Alma and slipped his arms around her, something else that should have been shocking but wasn't. Just the resident ghost, after all. *The resident ghost who can really kiss.* Bart's touch tingled with cold fire.

"Well, hello," Alma said.

"I missed you," said Bart, then he put his mouth over hers and kissed her. She felt something feathery— his chest touching hers—and she nearly dissolved into it. His tongue was cool in her mouth, and full of sparks. He tasted almost sweet.

Alma stepped back for a moment and looked into his bronze-flecked eyes. They were almost exactly level with her own as they stood facing each other. Bart kissed her again, and his mouth poured her full of prickly, contagious electricity. It was hard to pull away from him. He slipped a hand into her sweater under her bra, and cupped her left breast.

"Let me," he whispered. "Please." His fingers were gentle. He found her nipple and stroked it. "Oooo," he said.

A bolt of electricity shot through Alma and landed between her legs.

He kissed her again, harder, still playing with her

nipple. Another sharper electric bolt. She stepped backward to lean against the wall, feeling the weightlessness of him glittering on her, yet feeling his shirt and the buttons of his knickers. His hips rubbed against hers, but they weren't hips, exactly. They were neither firm nor soft. They were just there—and fiery. He pressed against her and didn't at the same time.

"Wow. Maybe I should, um, brush my teeth," she said at last. His hand was still on her breast, but then he let go.

"If you like," he said.

Alma realized she was trembling as she tried to steady herself for the walk to the bathroom. *I'm about to... I don't know, but whatever it is, I'm about to do it with a ghost. If we actually can manage to... Well, at least I've still got my IUD...* But that was silly. How could a ghost get you pregnant?

Back in the bedroom, Bart had lit the candles and was sitting on her bed. He smiled as she walked toward him, and his bronze-brown eyes glowed in the candle light. He'd taken his hair out of its queue and it flowed like a shadow over his shoulders, which were just slightly translucent.

"When you kissed me last night, the lights in this whole house went out," said Alma. "And then you disappeared. But tonight..."

"That won't happen again. Can't you tell? I've been practicing," said Bart. He was unbuttoning his shirt. His chest was luminous, of course, but also very well-muscled. There was a small, odd scar over his heart—just a few inches across.

"Practicing?" said Alma.

"Not on anyone else, don't worry," said Bart, and his face lit up, too. He was smiling. "This is all a matter of control, just as it is in the flesh." He chuckled. "It has been *so* long…" He tossed his shirt on the floor. "Come here, my dove."

My dove. Alma sat next to him, and he pulled her sweater over her head and then gazed at her. "Oh, my," he said. "You *are* ravishing."

"No one ever called me ravishing before," said Alma as Bart fumbled with her bra.

"*These* things," he said. "I have no experience…"

"Hooks … in the back," she said. He found them and gently slid the straps off her shoulders.

"So I see," he said. "Lay back."

She did, and Bart tugged gently at her leggings.

"A button and a zipper. Over on the side. You know what a zipper…"

But Bart already had undone it. "I do keep up, you know. Zippers are simpler," he said. He tugged off her leggings, threw them on the floor, and lay down on his side next to her, propped up an elbow. "Oh, my dear," he said again, and bent over her breast. "I must…" He stroked her nipple again and then gently nibbled it.

Alma closed her eyes. It was like being surrounded by the opposite of "a greater darkness." Bart ran his tongue down her stomach and Alma opened her eyes to see a silver line of sparks following it. Each one of them icy-hot. When he got to her panties, he pulled them down and opened her.

Now, Bart looked like a lantern in human form, glowing bright as fire, his knee britches still on. She felt him put his tongue to her and gently lick—once, twice… She closed her eyes and moaned. His hands were cool underneath her, lifting her up to his mouth. His tongue so, so cool! And she was very wet, hot wet from inside herself and chilly from the air in the room and Bart's sweet, smooth tongue. *I could actually come now. That's way, way too fast … is he still touching my breasts? He can't be, but I feel him there, too…*

He set her back down, slipped a finger into her and moved it slowly in and out. She wasn't coming, but she arched her back. His tongue ran back up her stomach and he nipped at her other breast, then licking her neck and kissing her again. She tasted herself in his kiss, something she never liked before, but he slid another finger into her and pinched a nipple with his other hand, still kissing her. More icy-hot sparks continued to seduce her. It was like diving into cold water, but wanting to be colder and colder. She tried to hold back and she didn't want to. She was absolutely going to…

Bart made an odd sound, a little like the wind blowing.

"Go ahead, Bart," she said. "It's okay. *You* should…" But Bart put his face between her legs again and opened her a little more so that he could suck at her tenderest part. *I'm freezing to death, but I want to,* she thought. *I want to! Dear God!* He slid a finger back into her.

Then she was lost. There were waves of cold flame inside her and outside her. She opened her mouth and no sound came out, and then she was shaking. Bart sucked more and it kept happening—and stopped—and built up again. And again. For a moment, Alma thought she had blacked out. She hadn't. She opened her eyes, still trembling, still coming a little, shivering.

Bart lay beside her. He took her hand and guided it to the bulge in his britches, and she stroked it. They lay that way for a few minutes.

"Bart?" she said at last. "*You.* You didn't. You should totally…"

"Enough, Alma," he said. "Do not tempt me further." He kissed her hand and laid it back down beside her.

"Tempt you?" said Alma. "But it's *okay!* And besides, you were the one who…"

"I shouldn't." He was still glowing, but his smile was a little sad. "Not that I *can't*. God, the living are—perfectly delicious!"

"Why can't you?"

"Because there would be … certain consequences for me. Mind you, I think *you'd* be all right."

What does that mean? Alma wondered if she should be angry, but she was still shivering. "You really thought I might *not* be?"

"No," said Bart. "It's just that the living are different and I'm, well, I'm not among them." Alma sat up and saw her reflection in the mirror across the room with its three candles flickering—and Bart's reflection glowing beside her. She was exhausted, but also relaxed—more relaxed than she'd been since… Well, since the first few days of her marriage, when she was still in love. But she wasn't in love. She knew that for certain.

She was incredibly cold, and now it didn't feel electric anymore. Alma pulled back the sheets and the quilt, holding them up so that Bart could slip under them beside her.

"I'm freezing!"

He chuckled.

"What's so funny?" she asked.

"Nothing, really. I don't get cold. I'll keep you company, though." It was strange to be able to see the barest outline of her pillow through his shoulders.

Chapter Seven

Alma and Bart sat up in her big yellow sleigh bed, propped up on pillows watching MTV. Alma had made herself a cup of Red Zinger herb tea and honey, and she sipped the last of it.

"She calls herself *Madonna*?" Bart shook his head.

"I think I like her," said Alma. "Good dance music, anyway. Although I guess that's not what you'd think of as dance."

"It's odd looking. But better than what the last residents of these rooms did when they put *The Grateful Dead* on the phonograph." He grimaced. "I'll admit I was intrigued by the name of that musical group, but they did not inspire a graceful gavotte."

"A graceful gavotte!" Alma laughed and waved her arms loosely over her head. "Did it look like that?"

"Exactly. Artless. Not that *you* ever could be, my dear Alma."

They watched Madonna dance in front of a wall of lights for a few minutes, and then Bart sighed. "Ah, Alma. I *do* wish I had dared to… Do you remember that I told you that ghosts sometimes lose each other because we … *dissipate*?"

"Yes."

"Well, I don't mean to be indiscreet but I've had a few lovers since I've been dead. Ghosts, of course. There was a Puritan woman—dead for a number of years before I met her—Tace Carson. She'd been on her way to get a boat down the river to New York and fell from her horse. She was my first, but I *certainly* was not hers. Puritans are not what you have been taught, m'lady. Tace was no prude." He chuckled. "She and I enjoyed each other. But she always warned me not to go-off—and was careful to stop just before that crucial point in love-making herself. That is by far, the greatest sadness about being on my side of things."

"Go-off. *Come*, you mean? So you can't…"

He nodded. "I'm not making you jealous by speaking of others, am I?"

"I don't know," said Alma. And that was true, she didn't. Strangeness upon strangeness—first having made love with a ghost, and then considering his other ghostly affairs.

"Tace … *dissipated*." Bart said.

"Which means?"

"Which means, which means… The last time we were together, I was pleasuring her as I did you. I was being careful to hold myself back. Tace begged me again and again not to stop, even though I reminded her it was unwise. At last, she was quite consumed by ecstasy and grew lighter and lighter in my arms until she turned into a sort of violet-scented mist…"

"What do you think happened?"

"Perhaps she went to the next place. Ghosts only have so much energy. I never see *anyone* from before 1680 these days."

"So you can't *come?* I mean, go-off. That's horrible. You must be incredibly frustrated."

Bart wrapped his arms around Alma again. "Frustrated by the sweetness of what we just did and the chance to do it again? I can do for you what I never could for Tace. Or rather, what I could do for her only that one, last time."

Alma shook her head. If you were going to dissolve into a mist, she could think of worse ways to do it.

But then she remembered Geoff Brussy. In the crazy rush of everything that had happened, in the sheer strangeness of it all, she'd forgotten about his teasing conversation and what he'd let happen to her bread order. *Turkey*, she thought, and wondered if that was the correct term for seriously annoying ghost.

"Bart," she said. "I met Geoff Brussy. Down at the school where I work."

"Oh, dear. I'd imagined you might." He kissed Alma on the cheek, and then looked down at the quilt. "I do hope you don't mind that I ... I bragged a bit to an old friend. Or rather, a very old enemy who has become a friend. Although he was a friend before he was an enemy ... it's so complicated. Things change in the decades after one ... you know."

After one dies, Alma thought. She was careful not to say it. But thinking about Geoff still ticked her off. "Yeah. He seemed to know what was going on. He put the bread I'd ordered for breakfast for the kids out where the raccoons would get it. He thought that was pretty hilarious."

"Sounds like Geoff. Always the trickster."

"He was your enemy?"

"Actually, he killed me," said Bart. "But I killed him, too, so we were equally inconvenienced."

"*Inconvenienced?*"

"Well, that's all it really is almost two hundred years after the fact, m'lady." Bart sighed again. "We'd both be quite dead anyway."

"You two *killed* each other? Oh, I get it. Not in a duel?"

Bart nodded. "Stupid, really. Neither one of us truly meant any real harm."

"Then why did you fight a *duel*?"

"Geoff was engaged to a lady who deserved far better. He was spending most of the hours he wasn't running his mill in bed with a strumpet named Polly

Verplank and he didn't take much care to hide the affair. I made a jest about Polly in the tavern. Geoff's humor being of the lowest variety, I thought he'd laugh, but he was in his cups."

"And so he challenged you?" said Alma.

"You have to understand that most people who fought duels didn't die. You'd bring a second with you, and a doctor, and usually one person would get somewhat injured. Then, it was over, your honor was intact, and that was that. Of course, most people used firearms. You have no idea how inaccurate they used to be. Although neither of us were much practiced with them, Geoff *insisted* upon swords. More gentlemanly, he said. He ran me through when we'd barely begun, so of course I did the same for him. He lasted until the next day. I died on the spot."

"That's horrible!"

"It happened a very long time ago," said Bart.

"God, it must have really *hurt*," said Alma. The Madonna video was over now and *The New Frontier* by Donald Fagan was on. Alma watched as it showed a pair of teenagers sneaking into their parents' fallout shelter. *Ugh.* Fallout shelters. The video was supposed to be making fun of the atom bomb jitters of the early sixties, but people were worried about it again. Ronald Reagan. Russia. *We could all end up ghosts.*

"I don't remember it hurting," said Bart. "I don't remember dying, either. I just ... found myself changed. On the other side, as people say now. But Geoff and I refought that duel about fifty times before we were done with it. I mean, *after* we had—you know."

Alma nodded. "When you were already ghosts."

"It was like neither one of us could believe what happened," said Bart. "But of course we couldn't do much harm to each other by then. So it was actually rather amusing. It passed the time, anyway. Although it also burned energy we could have used for … more pleasant activities. Neither of us understood that for a while. " He smiled, and glanced at the TV screen. "What's this song about?"

"About a time maybe twenty years ago," said Alma. "Actually, I like it a lot."

Bart gently pulled her over to his side of the bed and ran a hand down her back.

He kissed her and she felt the same icy-hot jolt she did the first time, but then he pulled away.

"Oh, dear. I really am much more tired than I'd anticipated," he said. "I'm afraid I must…" Bart became more and more transparent, until all that Alma could see was his shirt. Then the lights in her apartment went off.

She sat in her dark bedroom for a few moments wondering if Bart had actually dissipated before she realized how much she hoped he hadn't. She ran a hand through her hair, which crackled with static electricity. Alma heard her landlord's heavy step coming up the stairs and knew she'd better get a bathrobe on—and *fast*.

Chapter Eight

The phone was ringing and the light in Alma's window looked like late morning. *Oh, shit*, she thought for a moment, and then remembered it was Saturday and she hadn't overslept. Everything that had happened the night before raced back to her. It was … completely weird. But maybe not bad-weird.

Sex with a ghost. And I didn't dream it. She rolled over and grabbed the telephone beside her bed. It was Mary.

"I just wanted to make sure you were okay after last night," she said. "I feel kind of responsible for that nonsense in the bar. You seemed bummed when you left our place."

"I wasn't," said Alma. "What I can't believe is that you and Cleo were okay with all that stupid, stupid crap Jan was going on about. I had no idea he was such a jerk about stuff."

"Straight guys—they say things like that sometimes. They don't get that they're being major assholes. It's like they think they have the right. I thought *you'd* be upset about him and Jessie," Mary said. "Seriously. She was being flirty with him at work, but she's usually flirty. I really did not see that coming."

Alma cackled. "Worst possible case scenario, it burns out and they still have to work together. Happens."

"You're not … disappointed?"

"Over *Jan?* Oh, c'mon. He *works* for me."

"Hah," said Mary. "I was thinking, you know, with the divorce finally coming through, you'd want to tip a few back and be shameless."

"Shameless?" said Alma, "*Moi?*" She sat up and stretched. It actually felt kind of great.

"Yeah, shameless!" said Mary's voice, from the place above Alma's head where she was holding the phone.

Alma brought the receiver back to her mouth. "I'm *never* shameless!" She thought again about what *else* had happened the night before. "Never, ever! Especially not with good looking lunkheads I have to work with."

"Well, that's excellent to know," said Mary. "You sound the opposite of bummed, actually."

"That's because I am," said Alma. "Hey, I want to stick my head in at the kitchen just to make sure everything's going okay, but you want to hike The Upper Trail this afternoon? I've never done it, and I keep hearing about it. Would Cleo be into it? I'll grab some lunch to bring along from Marty's."

"Girl, you have to stop worrying about work so much! The orders are all in, and you've got the shifts covered, right? Lots of kids went home anyway."

"Right. We were down about twenty as of last night's dinner."

"So, menu's posted. You've got us staffed up. I bet that guy Max who had your gig before you didn't spend his weekends worrying. Yeah, let's go hike. Cleo went down to Beacon to see her mom, but I'd love some exercise. Got me some Garbage Pie to work off."

"I seem to recall that I put a good dent in that vile thing myself," said Alma.

By noon, they were hiking an uphill near the river. The Upper Trail was perfect for late October— steep enough to be a sweaty walk, but the cool air and the golden autumn light changed things—more or less.

"Phew!" said Mary. "I think it's like a quarter of a mile before the big payoff view." She took off her oversized neon green sweater and tied it around her neck.

"I can make it. You need water? There's Perrier in my backpack. Picked it up when I got lunch."

"Oh, fancy! Let's wait 'till we can sit down and enjoy things. I swiped a couple of your muffins from yesterday and brought 'em along. Those were good."

"Hah!" said Alma, and thought of Geoff.

They walked on quietly for a while, their hiking boots crunching on the gravel path. Just as they passed a brilliantly red maple tree, its leaves shimmering in the wind, they saw the stopping-off point with a few well-shaded benches facing the water. The view was spectacular. The Hudson River glittered a million different shades of blue, green, and brown, with the trees equally vivid in mostly red and yellow. The lighthouse stood on its little island near the opposite shore. A small armada of sailboats were out for one of the last weekends before their owners would put them in dry dock for the winter. It was cool under the trees, and Mary slipped back into her sweater as Alma spread out the takeout containers on the bench between them.

"Put that chicken salad down over here!" said Mary. "Oh! You got tabouli, too. Fabulous!"

"Marty's actually makes good tabouli," said Alma. "I keep thinking I should make some at work, but I'm not sure the kids would go for it."

"Maybe if you called it something else," said Mary. Her mouth was full and she grabbed a napkin.

Alma stood up and looked down the river. "So you *can't* see the castle on Bannerman's Island from up here," she said. "Bummer. Cool looking place, like a castle. I guess we're too far north for that."

"That's way down by *Fishkill*," said Mary. "You're not from here, girl. Want some more chicken salad? 'Cause I'm going to kill it all if you don't. Grapes and almonds and curry! God, I am ravenous!"

"Fight you for the grapes," said Alma. "Fishkill. Yeah, I guess that's right. I used to pass it on the train on my way back to New Paltz from Westchester. I always wondered about Bannerman's."

"I think it was actually just a place for storing gunpowder and stuff, like in the eighteen hundreds or something. An armory. There are ghost stories, though. The Indians thought that island was full of spirits. I've also heard something about a sunken ship that still tolls its bell…"

Ghost stories. Alma couldn't help it. She giggled.

"What's funny?" said Mary. "We should eat some muffins. Someone really talented made them."

Alma did not want to giggle again. But she did.

"Okay, okay. Now you're going to have to tell me."

"Oh, nothing," said Alma. "Probably just, you know, the stress of the divorce being over now. Relief." She held out a paper cup. "Hit me up with some more of the Perrier."

"Here ya go," said Mary. The wind blew and the river glimmered.

Alma tipped back her mineral water and grinned broadly. "It is so *gorgeous* up here," she said. "Just … glorious! What a beautiful, beautiful day."

Mary looked Alma hard in the face. "You know, if I hadn't known you were heading straight home from our place last night…"

"What?"

"I could swear…"

"*What?*"

"Oh, I don't know. That something *fabulous* has happened to our Alma. Recently. As in last night."

"Really." Alma tried to sound matter-of-fact, like—well, the boss lady—and she almost pulled it off.

But then she giggled again—and was furious with herself. She couldn't tell Mary, of all people. *But who do I tell?* She silently answered her own question—nobody. You do not go around telling people you just fell into a red-hot affair with a *ghost*. You especially don't tell a coworker a story like that one week from Halloween! Even if she is an old friend. You end up sounding like Benny the Beemer if you do that.

But then Alma thought of something else. *Benny the Beemer seems pretty darn happy, especially when no one is reminding him that he's being inappropriate. It would be nice to have someone to tell ... it really would. Mary is cool...*

These days, Alma didn't have much in the way of close friends. Most of the people she'd hung out with when she was married ended up on her ex's side of the divorce. They were friends of Stefan, couples, other faculty wives who asked for her pasta al forno recipe and smiled indulgently as she wrote it out. "Stefan tells me you write *poetry*, too!" Except she wasn't—writing poetry, that was.

These days, Alma's friends were fellow kitchen rats—who worked for her.

My life, is my job. Well, mostly, anyway. And then she tried not to drift into a fantasy about Bart. It was nice having someone who demanded nothing from her— even if he was not quite of this world. But a ghost? And what was that scary comment he'd made about her probably being all right after... *What, exactly, did I do last night?*

"Wow, Alma! What is *up* with you?" said Mary. "Now you almost look like you could cry."

"Do I?"

"As a matter of fact, yeah."

"As a matter of fact, I *could* cry," said Alma.

"But I don't want to. It's messy."

"Is it the divorce?"

Alma nodded. That was a piece of the truth.

"I think I have Kleenex," said Mary.

Alma blinked hard, inwardly vowing she would not need Kleenex.

They watched the boats on the river. A few big dark birds circled in the wind far above them. "Wow," Alma said, pointing. "Are those eagles?"

"In *Englehook*?" said Mary. "Buzzards. They say the red-tailed hawks might come back if we get things cleaned up a little more, though. Yay for Pete Seeger and the Clearwater! Probably there's a dead deer around somewhere."

"Poor thing," said Alma. "Oh, well." She sniffled again, and went back to watching the buzzards. "Mary?" she said, "I'm having an affair with a *ghost*."

"Oh, yeah. I totally get it. Metaphor for your marriage, right? All dead and…"

"No. No metaphor." The wind blew a few brilliant red maple leaves into Alma's lap, and not knowing what else to do, she picked one up and pretended to examine it. Neither of them said anything for a minute.

Mary examined Alma's face again, carefully. "A *ghost*?"

Alma nodded. "Yup."

"Wow. You're not kidding, are you?"

"Nope," said Alma. "I'm not." There was another silence.

"So. Um, what's that like?"

Alma brightened. "Well, the sex is *mind*-blowing, actually. Kind of mentholated-chilly. But it feels great!"

"The *sex*. Ghosts can…?"

"Apparently. They don't usually pair up with …

the living, though."

"The living." Mary put a hand over her mouth.

"I'm *not* nuts, Mary," said Alma. "Really. I know I'm not nuts. Because... Okay, his name is Bartholomew. And he likes to be called Bart. He lives—or I guess the word is "stays" in my apartment. Because, you know, he's not *living*, even though, well... And his friend, Geoff Br—"

"Oh, my *God!*" said Mary. "Alma!! Brussy. Geoffrey Brussy. And Bartholomew—would that be Bartholomew Addison Jenkins? You're *really* not from here, are you? Downstate girl. Holy crap!"

"You know who they are? Bart—I mean Bartholomew..."

Mary nodded, hard. "He killed..."

"They killed *each other*," said Alma. "In a duel..."

"A duel that used to get *reenacted* for the local school kids every October. Guys from the local historical society dressed up in knee knickers with swords. There was plenty of fake blood. When I was in high school, they found some old letters. Turned out the whole thing was about some dumb shit barroom insult—had nothing whatsoever to do with Tories and Patriots still pissed off after the Revolution. But for anyone our age who grew up in Englehook... Holy *shit,* Alma. We used to have a picnic afterward and everything."

"A *picnic*?" said Alma.

"They can be pleasant this time of year," said Mary, packing up their empty deli containers.

"I've noticed," Alma said.

"Wow," said Mary. "It even kind of makes sense that Bartholomew would be hanging out up on your end of town. The historical society did the reenactment down by Englehook Primary, but they told us it wouldn't have been fought downtown because duels happened in out-of-the-way places. So as not to get busted, you know? Geoffrey Brussy's mill was on the site of Bright Day School, by the way. I always figured that was why everyone said the main building is haunted and stuff."

"You don't think I'm nuts, then?"

"I'm not saying *that!*" Mary laughed. "Do tell me more."

"Only if you—God, Mary, you can't be talking about this to everyone!"

"Obviously I can't be talking about this to *anyone!* Well, maybe Cleo, but she is silent as the tomb, ha-ha."

"Ha-ha?"

"Joke. Bad joke. Cleo won't tell anyone. This is some first class, A-number-one insane stuff. I don't know why I believe you, but I do. I guess you don't seem … I don't know … delusional."

Alma laughed. "I work hard. Maybe I work too hard to be delusional."

"It's not work. You're too *serious* to be delusional—or that kind of delusional, anyway. You're too focused. I mean, you're arty and everything—everyone in Englehook is arty—but you're not all spacey woo-woo. Airy-fairy. Like that."

"Oh, *good*," said Alma. "I'd hate to be all spacey woo-woo. You really want to hear more?"

"*Yes!*" said Mary. She put her elbows on her knees and propped her chin in her hands. "Please!"

"Okay. I've actually chatted with his pal Geoff a bit. At the school. I can see why someone might want to stick a sword in him. He put our bread order out and raccoons got into it. On purpose. Speaking of bad jokes. That one was on me because he knew what happened with Bart. Hilarious. Or he thought so. That's why I had to bake—"

"*These!*" said Mary, pulling a baggie out of her backpack. "And here are the last two! Want one?"

"Oh, sure," said Alma. She poured herself some more Perrier. They ate their muffins and watched the river for a few minutes.

"They're really delicious," said Mary. "And holy shit."

"Thanks. It's the fresh nutmeg from the health food co-op."

"Makes a difference," said Mary. "So. A ghost. And he's … um … *good.*"

"Yup," said Alma. "*Really* good."

Chapter Nine

On Sunday night, Alma spread the paperwork out on her bed and went over the week's menu. Pancakes on Monday morning. The kids would love that. Maybe she'd make them super happy and do hamburgers and fries for lunch, too, an easy start to the week. She could sneak the missing veggies into the stew at dinner. Had she ordered buns for the burgers, and a little whole wheat bread for the peanut butter and jelly sandwiches always available for anyone not in the mood for the main course? Check and check.

Halloween was going to be the following Sunday. Lots of kids would be gone over that weekend. Alma wanted to make sure there was happy-making food on that day for the kids stuck at school. Fried chicken— yeah. Mary had volunteered to do dinner that night and she was good with the fry-o-later. Jan often worked Sunday nights, but he would be needed at the bar on Halloween.

Thank God for Mary. Because Alma wasn't going to have anything to do with work on Halloween. If you were having a red-hot affair with a ghost, maybe you wanted to be … a little *available* that day.

There was only one problem—Alma's apartment had been very quiet Saturday and all of Sunday, too. No Bart, not even a hint of him. The whole thing was beginning to feel like a hopeful date that turned out to be just a one-nighter. The ghost version of never calling back.

Her only visitor the rest of the weekend had been Peter Koslov, her landlord. "We put 'em in new circuit breaker for your apartment," he said. "Electrician. No more lights out. Mama says you're good girl." This time,

Peter simply handed her the kielbasa, instead of leaving it in her refrigerator. That was funny but it made her feel a little guilty, which was ridiculous. The house actually needed a new circuit breaker and a whole lot of electrical work besides. Bart hadn't really *meant* to short circuit the lights in the building.

She pulled herself out of bed early to do breakfast on Monday morning, not quite in the mood to work with Jessie. *God knows what kind of weekend she and Jan had, but I bet I will know, in full-screen Technicolor, by about 11 AM. Oh, joy.* She showered, gelled her wild blonde hair into quasi-submission and pulled on her jeans, buttoning them over a nicely worn-out, hugely oversized men's shirt. It had thick purple and black stripes on it, and looked very cool with its sleeves rolled up. Best thing she'd ever scored at the Grace Church thrift shop.

"Bart?" she called quietly into the pre-dawn darkness in her apartment just before she left. No answer.

Alma drove down the hill to Bright Day. There had been rain the day before, and more leaves were down, like orange and red stars on the shiny black road. She pulled into her parking space, turned off her headlights and ignition, and took a minute for a pre-walking-into-work deep breath. As she closed her car door, a form took shape in the pre-dawn murk. Geoff, pipe in hand, glowed a dull yellowish-green. He waved and walked across the parking circle toward her.

Alma's stomach tightened. She looked around to see if there were any stray childcare workers—or worse, Benny the Beemer—up a few minutes early to see her talking to what would appear to be no one. But Big Dan the OD (OD stood for Overnight Duty) wasn't even in front of Sundog Cottage, smoking his morning English Oval. She and Geoff were all alone. Geoff looked solemn.

"Alma!" he said. "I have a message for you of great importance."

Shit. "Bart's all right, isn't he?"

Geoff's serious expression melted. "Oh, he'd *love* that! You were worried*!* I bet you think he's *dissipated!* From what I understand, it might have been a very near thing, you naughty lass." He winked. "Bart's fine."

Oh, God. Could Bart manage to keep anything to himself? *But I needed to tell someone, too. I guess he's allowed.*

"And the message is?"

"That you wore him out. Not that he didn't appreciate it. You'll see him soon enough."

"Oh, good." Alma surprised herself by feeling relieved—and hopeful. Except it was mildly annoying hearing the news from Geoff. *Naughty lass, indeed! What else does he know?* "Thank you, Geoff. This morning's bread order, I see, has been left safely inside. Thank you for your restraint."

Geoff chuckled. "You'll need the bread. Especially since you happen to be out of flour."

"I'm not out of flour."

"Oh, yes you are, m'lady fair. Not a bit left. Flour is the funniest stuff. It just ... *disappears* sometimes. A miller knows about such things." He opened his non-pipe-holding hand to reveal a handful the stuff—and blew it in the direction of her face. Then he chuckled again and vanished.

Alma changed into her whites and checked the stockroom. Dammit! Geoff was right, despite the fact she'd had at least half a bin left after she'd made the corn bread on Friday. No one else had baked all weekend. And were those dusty white footprints on the floor? *Geoffrey ... you jerk!*

So much for pancakes. But yeah, there *was* bread. So, French toast.

Benny the Beemer came in as she was cracking eggs and laying bacon out on trays for the oven.

"We need syrup on the tables, Benny," she said.

Benny's eyes lit up. "Pancakes and bacon!" he said, as he put on his apron. He made a growly-engine noise. "That's going to feel good in my—"

"Hey. Let's stay ... appropriate," said Alma. "Besides, it's French toast, actually."

"Oh, wow. Roy's going to *hate* that." Benny frowned. Roy was Benny's new roommate. Roy had long red hair. He could instantly calculate what day of the week your birthday would be a hundred years from now. He couldn't read. And he was obsessed with Paul McCartney and Wings.

"That's silly, Benny," said Alma. "Roy doesn't hate anything. Roy is the sweetest kid here. Besides, who doesn't like French toast?"

"Roy doesn't. He *really* doesn't. He hates French toast because it's not pancakes. It's part of his Theory of All Food." Benny was pouring syrup from a big plastic bottle into the table-sized pitchers.

"Well, he can have oatmeal, then. Or corn flakes. Or PBJ. There's always cold cereal, too. Roy he doesn't hate *bacon*, does he?"

"I don't know." Benny put the pitchers into a bus bin to carry them into the dining rooms, merrily making car-going-around-a-corner-very-fast noises as he hurried the syrup onto the tables. Alma almost scolded him, but then she stood at the kitchen's side door, watching him gleefully do his job. *Let him be happy*, she thought, and turned on the radio instead.

By serving time, the dining rooms smelled of bacon and syrup, and the French toast was puffing up nicely on the flat top. Alma liked cooking on the flat top. It made her feel like a diner cook from the 40s. She stood in front of it, flipping French toast with her long spatula, and dropping pieces of whole wheat bread into the egg, milk, maple syrup and vanilla extract mixture to soak. She put a knob of butter onto the flat top and added another few slices of soaked bread when it sizzled. The kids were hungry, and the child care staff was eating heartily, too. Sun had broken through the clouds outside and the morning light in the kitchen windows was yellow with October leaves.

Benny brought her three empty stainless steel serving trays and set them down beside her with a clatter. She filled them and he ran them to the service window. "French toast!" he called into the dining rooms, then he hurried back to her. "Uh-oh."

"Uh-oh? What's uh-oh?" said Alma, humming along with the radio. *Come On, Eileen* was on. She liked that song. It fit her sunny mood.

"Roy was just here," said Benny. "He ran outside. He didn't eat anything. He looked mad."

"So he really *does* hate French toast," said Alma. "I guess I could send a little something to his classroom later, poor guy. Who's on for you today?" Alma hated to think of anyone hungry. "Are there more trays at the window? Go look."

"Two more trays," said Benny. "And I have to get orange juice. I don't know why you'd drink orange juice with French toast. It tastes really sour." He walked back from the window with the trays and took an empty juice pitcher to the giant vat of frozen OJ they mixed up every morning.

"Yeah, not fair, huh, Benny? Orange juice should always taste sweet," Alma said.

Someone started shouting in the hall outside the

kitchen's back door. "No! No! No! There were no pancakes! Why?"

The door slammed open, and Roy was in it. He wasn't a very imposing fifteen-year-old—skinny, really. He was wearing a washed-out Wings Over America t-shirt and he was white-faced with rage.

"Alma!" he yelled. "*No pancakes!* The chalkboard said pancakes and there were no pancakes! Why don't you make *pancakes*, Alma?"

Benny began to make a noise like squealing brakes.

Alma put down her spatula. "Benny, that's inappropriate," she said. "And Roy, you're being inappropriate, too. That was very rude. I was, um, out of flour."

Benny stopped. Roy didn't.

"French *toast!*" he shouted, and then he turned it into a chant. "Frenchtoastfrenchtoast!" It could have been funny—or horrifying. Alma decided that it was both.

She stuck her head into the dining hall. "Child care?" she called. "Anyone around from Saturn Cottage?" A woman about Alma's age with long, curly black hair trotted over to the serving window and stuck her head in. Judy Fleming.

Roy was still chanting. "Frenchtoastfrenchtoast!"

"Oh, crap," said Judy. "Yeah. He says he hates the stuff." She ran into the kitchen through the side door, pulling out her walkie-talkie. "Child care to kitchen," she said into it. "Roy, stop that! You'll get behavior points off!"

"Child care to kitchen! A *million zillion* points off!" yelled Roy. Alma spun around. Roy was about three inches from her face, a two pound loaf of whole wheat bread poised over his shoulder like a baseball bat.

"Put down the bread, Roy," said Alma. Judy was attempting to loop her arms around his shoulders.

"*French toast!*" bellowed Roy, and squirmed away from Judy. He brought the loaf of bread down over Alma's toque. Its wax paper wrapping broke in two and slices of whole wheat cascaded over her shoulders and fell onto the floor. It was shocking, but didn't hurt. *Okay, now this is funny. But I can't laugh!* She chewed the inside of her lip.

Roy's eyes were still wild.

"Roy!" said Judy, "I'm disappointed! That was … *so* inappropriate."

"French *toast!*" muttered Roy.

Three large male child care workers flew in the back door of the kitchen. "Quiet room?" one asked.

"Nah," said Judy. Roy was standing next to her silently, now. "I'll walk it off with him. You okay, Alma? He didn't hurt you, did he?"

"With a Pullman loaf of sliced whole wheat bread?" said Alma. "Not possible." She started picking up the slices that had hit the floor and tossing them into the garbage. Breakfast service was most of the way over by then, but there were a few empty trays waiting at the window. "I think I've got enough left on the flat top for the last few kids. Might need someone from child care to run to the bakery to pick up bread for PBJ subs. Yikes."

Benny skipped over to the service window for the trays. "*Rrum, rruumm, ruumm,*" he said. Alma and Judy exchanged glances, and Judy shrugged.

"You're on the *job*," said Judy to Benny, and he stopped. "C'mon, you," she said to Roy, who was now staring at the floor. They went out the open back door. Jessie walked in as they left, stooping to pick up the last dozen pieces of bread.

"Morning, Alma," she said. "Holy crap. What

happened here?'

"Roy doesn't like French toast," said Benny. "He hit Alma with *bread*. He's my roommate."

"I *hate* French toast!" yelled Roy, from the hall outside the kitchen and Alma started laughing.

Geoffrey, she thought. *I'd kill him myself if he weren't already dead.*

"You know, I never told you when you first came to work here, but Max always used to keep that back door locked during meal service."

That was suddenly hilarious, and Alma laughed harder. It took her a while to stop.

"Well," she said finally. "Burgers for lunch. And fries. I'll do a salad but no one will eat it. Want to make some of that fudge sauce you were talking about last week? Maybe even sneak some real sugar in? We could let them have ice cream sundaes for dessert."

"Sure!" said Jessie, and smiled a suspiciously huge smile. "I happen to have the world's most fabulous boss. You really okay and everything?"

Alma beamed back at her. "I'm just hunky-dory. And I'll bet *you* had a great weekend."

"Oh. *Yeah*," Jessie said. "The best weekend ever."

Alma punched Jessie in the arm. "Hey, it's fine to have a great weekend. Everyone should have a great weekend."

"Including me," said Benny the Beemer, stacking trays for the dish machine. "I had a great weekend, too."

Chapter Ten

"So I hear you really *believe* in the ghosts," said Cleo, raising her eyebrows. She was sitting with Alma in Marty's, at one of the little round cafe tables in the deli and coffee shop's big window. Alma felt her cheeks burn. She stared at Cleo's big-shouldered black and white checked blazer and her chunky ebony beads.

"Guess I do," said Alma.

Cleo burst into a belly laugh and reached across the table to grab Alma's hand.

Alma had hoped to run a couple of errands after she got out of Bright Day and get back home as soon as she could. She found herself in a surprisingly funky mood. It was Wednesday, she hadn't seen a trace of Bart (still), and work was full of the amazing new love story of Jan and Jess. Jan was so considerate! So romantic! Even at work! It was really great, Jessie kept saying, to have an understanding boss who let her *talk* about it. And talk about it and talk about it...

To top it all off, Alma had bumped into Cleo, who wanted all the juicy details about ghostly lovemaking, firsthand.

"Hey. Trust me, I'm a social worker. I do understand the *confidential* stuff, ya know." Cleo grinned. "I can be ... silent as the tomb!"

Silent as the tomb. "Oh, please," she said. "Let's talk about non-spooky things. So far it's just a one-nighter, anyway."

"A blazing *hot* one-nighter with a..." Cleo dropped her voice. "...*ghost!*"

Englehook was a town that was serious about Halloween. It was currently bursting with pumpkins, Halloween costumes for sale, and bowls of candy by cash registers. Every shop window in town was decorated with paintings of ghouls and monsters, an annual art project from Englehook High. In fact, three teenagers were right at that moment painting a life-sized picture of two ghostly men dueling with swords on the outside of the very window where Alma and Cleo were sitting. *Oh, for the love of God.* She pointed at them. "Check *that* out."

Cleo turned around to look. "Oh my," she said. "Mmm, mmm, mmm. I didn't know ghosts bled red blood. What a coincidence. Bet you've heard all about *that* little disagreement."

"Yup," said Alma. *Bart.* She really wanted to go home. But suppose her apartment was as empty as it had been? *Geoff said he didn't dissipate. Could I have been seduced and abandoned by someone who isn't even alive?*

"It *is* kind of a disturbing image when you think about it," said Cleo.

"Mary says they used to *reenact* that duel here. For elementary kids."

"And then the little fourth-grade boys would *re*-reenacting it for the next month, high on their haul of mini-Snickers bars. Stickin' each other with pencils and gettin' sent to the nurse," said Cleo, shaking her head. "Anyway, give us a break. George Washington slept somewhere else. It's the only thing ever happened in this town. And you got yourself a ringside seat."

"I guess," said Alma.

Cleo drained her cappuccino and got up. "Look, I didn't mean to be all snoopy. Let's you and me and Mary get together *after* Halloween, okay?" She grinned again.

"Look. This … *thing* is actually pretty confusing, Cleo," Alma said. "Whatever it is."

Cleo hugged her. "I can only imagine," she said.

"Seriously. You doing okay?"

"Trying my best." She attempted a smile. "See you soon."

Alma was walking to her car when a man with long red hair streaming over his shoulders waved at her from the next block and began slowly jogging toward her. For one awful minute she thought it was Roy-who-hates-French-toast. But it was someone worse. Charlie Sassian, Board of Health Inspector.

"Ah, *fuck!*" Alma said under her breath.

But as Charlie got closer, it wasn't so bad. Out of his workday pigtail, his hair caught the autumn sun. He was wearing a long-sleeved tie-dyed t-shirt, jeans, and a nicely-scuffed up pair of cowboy boots.

Ha, an old hippie. Who'da thunk? She could almost hear what her ex-husband would have said. "The things you see when you don't have a gun." Hippies were a particular object of his scorn. It might even be worth going out with a hippie a few times just to imagine how horrified Stefan would be.

Charlie actually looks kind of good.

And that would have been interesting, if she weren't on her way home to what could possibly be a much *more* interesting evening with Bart ... unless, of course, the whole thing really *was* just a one-nighter.

"Alma," said Charlie. "It's been too long!"

"It's actually been less than a week," said Alma. "Hi."

"Less than a week is long enough. I *demand* that you have a cup of coffee with me. C'mon! I'll even entertain you." He pointed at what looked like a tiny guitar case slung over his shoulder.

"And that is a...?"

"Man-do-*line!*" Charlie sang joyfully. Alma remembered being in college and hearing the word sung that way on an album called *Tubular Bells* by Mike Oldfield. If you were planning on spending the evening on the receiving end of a bong, that record was just the ticket. Still, she felt a pang of nostalgia.

"Tubular *Bells*!" she sang back to him.

Charlie took her arm. "Just so," he said. "How fun is that record? And what a movie soundtrack. Let's you and me go to Marty's and…"

Why did the offer seem tempting? Alma sighed. "Oh, Charlie, I just got *out* of Marty's. And I'm … really beat, actually, and…" She thought about Bart again. "I have to get home."

"Oh. Well, that's disappointing," he said, and wiped an imaginary tear from one eye.

He has green eyes. Or are they blue? Or grey? I can't decide. That's the weird thing about green eyes…

"Here, then," said Charlie, and unzipped his mandolin case far enough to pull a flier out of it. It was for an open mic at The Cracked Bell, a pub a few blocks from The Old Fascist. "There's a jam session here on Thursday nights. I sit in on mando and sometimes on fiddle. Good tunes. You know—like The Burrito Brothers? Old And In The Way?"

Charlie the health department inspector is a hippie—and a wanna-be country rock musician. That's too wild. "Yeah," she said. "I kinda liked Old And In The Way. Girl in my dorm was super into them." Her thoughts drifted back to college again. So many friends, people knocking on each other's doors… Maybe that was her problem. Maybe she was just lonely.

"Come down tomorrow, then. I'll buy you a beer."

"I just might," Alma said. Her apartment suddenly seemed a bit less attractive. She immediately felt guilty. But she couldn't take a ghost to an open mic.

Or anywhere, really. *I didn't give Charlie a for-sure yes. Doesn't matter, I've got to get home.*

Chapter Eleven

Alma could hear her phone ringing on the other side of her locked apartment door. She juggled shopping bags and her pocketbook to dig out her key.

I don't know why I'm rushing. It's only going to be my mom again.

"Oh, Alma, I've been so concerned about you! I've been calling and calling. I kept leaving messages."

Yup. Mom all right. Alma held in her sigh. "You shouldn't worry so much, Mom. I mean, seriously…"

"It's Stefan. I'm afraid he's been on … a *bit* of a bender, dear. The divorce, you know."

"You told me that a couple of days ago." *Why does she call me when the person she's really worried about is my ex?* Alma put the bags down on the floor and balanced the phone receiver on her shoulder.

"I told you he got tipsy at dinner. One night. This is different. He's really…"

My mother's idea of "tipsy" means you need three people to carry you home. But she also knew what Stefan was capable of when he was out of control. It sounded like that's what her mother was trying to tell her. "How bad is he, Mom? Is he, like, missing work? Is he drunk *all* the time?"

"…and I've had such dreams!" Alma's mother said. Her voice shook.

"Mom, tell me what Stefan's doing."

"Well, he *did* miss work, dear. He says he can't live without you. I'm so afraid…"

"That…"

"That he'll crash his car or something. Or get fired. Or…"

"Mom, Stefan isn't my problem anymore. This is one of the big reasons why I left. I—"

"And I dreamed that you were … surrounded by a greater darkness again! Such a vast and enormous greater darkness!"

A vast and enormous greater darkness? Mom's really good at being melodramatic. But still…

"Mom," she said, "It doesn't help me when you say those things." That was true. But melodramatic or not—true or not—the whole thing with the greater darkness was actually scary. The kind of scary it was hard to stop thinking about. Sure, it sounded like patented Philomena-bullshit. But suppose it wasn't?

"Alma, last Friday night I couldn't sleep after the dream I had. There was a man. He was pulling you into a dark, dark carriage—like a hearse! He was going to drive away with you. I wanted to call you on Saturday and tell you about it but your father said I was being a damn fool and I should leave you alone. And then Stefan started calling *us*! I just couldn't bear it anymore."

"Mom," Alma said. "There's no dark carriage. There's no man. It was just a dream. And Stefan will have to work things out for himself." Her mother began to cry. Alma knew that there *was* a man—the ghost of one. A ghost that might possibly appear right now. After all, it *was* getting a little dark.

It took twenty minutes to get her mother off the phone—that and a promise to come down to Westchester and do Thanksgiving like a proper family for once. Alma put her milk and a fresh bottle of North Mountain Chablis in her refrigerator. Then she emptied out the old bottle—it made for a skimpy glass—and walked into the living room sipping it.

For a moment, thinking about Bart actually frightened her. *A hearse? But Mom exaggerates all the time. She's always made up stuff to win arguments. She's super full of herself and crazy.* Alma stood in front of her window with her wine, examining the bit of Hudson River that she could see since the maple down the street had dropped most of its leaves. The day was sinking into twilight and golden sun sparkled on the water.

I'm disgusting from having cooked hamburgers today. Alma always wondered how hamburger grease could work its way in under a chef's toque and into her hair. She finished her wine, headed for the bathroom, and turned on the shower. It took two serious latherings of Herbal Essance to blast the smell of the fryer and the burgers off her—that, and a big dose of conditioner to keep her wild curls from looking like Little Orphan Annie. Alma toweled off the steam from the mirror over her sink and carefully worked her wide-toothed comb through the tangles.

She was still in her bathrobe when the pounding started on her door.

"Alma, Alma!" This time, it wasn't her landlord. Alma dropped her comb, startled enough that her hands shook.

"Alma! Baby! I'm so, so sorry! I'm such a fucking asshole!" The voice was one she'd hoped she'd never hear again. Stefan's. She instantly felt nauseous. How the hell had he even gotten her address? He'd been so out of control when she'd told him she'd signed the lease on an apartment that she'd been careful to keep its location from him. That was the only thing she figured her loser lawyer had gotten right.

"Get out of here!" she yelled back. She knotted the belt of her robe tightly around her waist and walked into the living room.

"Please. Could we jus' talk?" The voice through the door was quieter now.

"Go home, Stefan," said Alma.

"I have no home without you, baby!" The door

rattled. "This was all a mistake! Please!"

And then, Alma felt a breeze behind her and a gentle pressure on her shoulders—Bart. His touch sparkled but it felt much colder than usual.

"Don't worry. Just … wait a minute. I'm gathering myself," he whispered.

"It's my ex-husband."

"I know who it is," said Bart. "Let him in."

"*What?*"

"Who's in there with you?" said Stefan. "I hear you talking to someone! Not that you wouldn't have the right. I'm just a no-good bastard," he wailed.

Yuck. Stefan was one disgustingly self-pitying drunk.

"Let him *in*," whispered Bart. "Go on. I'll defend you."

"*Defend* me?"

"On my honor as a gentleman," said Bart, squaring his luminous shoulders in his equally luminous white shirt.

"Will he even be able to *see* you?"

"He'll see me, all right. When the time is ripe." Bart smiled. Stefan was a pretty big wimp, anyway. *I could probably even take him down myself, especially drunk as he sounds. It would be kind of fun to see a ghost scare the snot out of him.*

"*Trust* me," said Bart. He wandered into the bedroom. "I'll be right back."

Alma opened the door. Stefan, in a pair of paint-splattered jeans and a washed-out black t-shirt, stood unsteadily in the hall. His hair was grayer than she remembered and looked filthy. Two cans of a Budweiser tall boy six-pack dangled from their plastic holder in his right hand and he reeked of the other four cans. He reeled into her living room and threw himself on the couch.

"Your apartment's … it's so *beautiful*," Stefan said. "God bless your sweet mother for telling me how to find you. Forgive me. Everything was my fault." And then he began to cry—big, loud hiccupping sobs. For about five seconds, Alma felt sorry for him. But then she was furious. *Your sweet mother. Jesus, Mom, really? Really?*

"Look, Stefan, I don't care whose fault it was. It's over. It's really over. And you can't stay here. In fact, you have to go right now, okay?"

"Why'd you let me in, then? C'mon. Sit down with me, baby." Stefan popped open one of the two remaining beers and stretched an arm out on the couch. "I heard you talking to somebody. Who's here?"

"She was talking to *me*, sir," said Bart in a loud voice. He marched into the room, and stepped in front of Alma. "You must stop bedeviling this woman."

"Whoa," said Stefan. He dropped his beer. It landed upright and foamed over. Alma picked it up. *This could be amusing.*

Stefan's expression was hard to read. He was pointing unsteadily at Bart. "You. You're a … um… What the fuck are you supposed to be, anyway? Halloween's not 'till Sunday." He staggered to his feet. "Act-shully, you look like kind of a pussy."

"Are you insulting me, sir?" said Bart.

"Are *you* screwing my wife?" said Stefan. "I'm not stupid. She's in her fucking bathrobe, ya know. And you just came outta the bedroom, right? Whoa. I can see through you, kinda. Oh, *shit*."

"No one talks to my lady that way," said Bart. "And may I point out that she is no longer your wife?"

"You happen to be *translucent*." Stefan belched, and then he laughed. "Hey. What the hell, Alma? The things you see when you don't have a gun!"

About time for him to trot out that one.

Alma felt another presence to the right of her, and saw a familiar greenish glow—Geoff.

"*Your* lady indeed, Bartholomew!"

"Whoa," said Stefan again, but this time in a smaller voice.

Geoff glared at Bart. "Thatch-gallows!"

"Dog-Booby!" said Bart.

Bart caught Alma's eye, and she saw he was trying hard not to laugh. Geoff pulled a long sword from a scabbard that hung at his side and suddenly there was one in Bart's hand as well.

Geoff waved his sword over his head and then he pointed its tip at Stefan.

"Explain your presence, sir! *You* have no place in this dispute!" said Geoff.

"Holy fuck," said Stefan, and dove behind the couch.

"Come out of there, sir! Come out!" shouted Bart. "You'll not be hiding back there! Have you no honor, cock robin?" Bart shoved the couch away from the wall, revealing Stefan crouched in the corner with his hands over his head.

Alma felt an elbow brush her side and turned to see Geoff smother a giggle, too. "Well may you be speaking of a man's honor, Bartholomew!" he said. "In front of your ... your *convenient!*" He caught Alma's eye again, and wiggled his eyebrows. A "convenient." That sounded kind of low rent. This was getting less amusing. Lots less amusing.

"My *convenient?*" Bart turned his gaze away from Stefan. "You, sir, shall learn the cost of those words!" He drew back his sword, flourished it, and plunged it deeply into Geoff's chest. An explosion of something shiny and the color of rust spattered the wall by her window, and soaked Geoff's shirt. Alma gasped, but she couldn't look away.

"Guh!" said Geoff, slumping forward onto Bart's sword. She watched him turn and stagger toward her ex-husband, drooling rusty slime down his chin. He heaved, spraying Stefan with it. Alma felt like heaving herself. She put a hand over her mouth. *This has got to be completely fake*, she thought. *They're already dead. But it's so gross…*

Bart stepped aside and took a theatrical bow, leaving his sword hilt-deep in Geoff. "In such a manner are villains repaid!" He glared at Stefan, who was wiping the gunk out of his nose with his fingers. Stefan's face was now white. The three-day drunk circles under his eyes looked almost black.

Geoff rocked back and forth, barely on his feet. "Oh! I am … slain," he croaked, spitting out another dark, viscous glob.

"Jesus!" shouted Stefan, and stumbled to his feet.

But then Geoff spun around on his toes and yanked the sword back out of his own chest. He skipped merrily over to Bart, swinging it over his head. "Take that, scoundrel!" Geoff said, and stabbed Bart so deeply the sword's tip emerged from his back.

"And so I die!" Bart coughed, and a flood of something that looked like mercury stained his shirt and splashed onto the floor. "But not before … I am … truly avenged!" He grabbed the sword that had been dangling from Geoff's hand and stabbed him a second time. Geoff clutched his chest and tumbled over, flat on his back.

Bart pulled back the dripping sword and lurched toward Stefan. "And now *you*, sir!"

Stefan burst out the door and thundered downstairs. Alma leaned against the wall, one hand still over her mouth. She realized she was still clinging to

Stefan's beer can with her other hand, hard enough to have dented it. It was very quiet for a moment. Then Bart began to laugh.

Geoff poked his head up. "Is he gone?"

"I think so," said Bart. "Oh, well done! Well done!" The sword still protruded from his chest and back. He reached a hand out and helped Geoff up off the floor.

"Thanks," said Geoff. "Allow me to remove this *murderous* implement." He pulled the sword out of Bart and snickered.

"Haha! Almost forgot about that!" Bart chuckled, slapped Geoff on the back, and they shook hands.

There was the sound of a car starting up outside. *Shit, he can't be driving*, Alma thought. *He's going to kill somebody, and it's going to be for real.* She felt too sick do anything about it.

Rust-colored and silver ghost-blood was splashed all over her floor and walls, and that wasn't a bit funny. Not at all. "Both of you," she said to Bart and Geoff. "Get the hell out of here. *Now.* I mean it."

"But we got *rid* of him for you," said Bart. He pulled a handkerchief from his pocket and quickly mopped up the multi-colored goo on the walls and the floor, plus the small puddle of beer from Stefan's can. Geoff pulled his shirt out of his britches and shook it a little. The rust-colored stains on it disappeared. "Thanks, old friend," Bart said to him, shaking the silver stains out of his own shirt.

"My *lady*," said Geoff, bowing to Alma and then he disappeared.

"Well," said Bart. "Now that we're *finally* alone… Good evening, my dear love. I said I'd defend you. Let us sit down together for some sweet conversation." He shoved the couch back where it belonged.

Alma's head spun. This was simply too much—the ridiculous, gory duel, Stefan's sudden appearance, her mother's interference in the whole thing and Bart's refusal to leave.

"Bart, I asked you to go, too. I meant it. I'm done."

"No. Please, Alma," said Bart.

She sat down on the couch and he bent over her to kiss her cheek. His lips were icy. "Bart, I said I *meant* it! You have to *go*. That was horrible," Alma said. "I can't be around stuff like that. I just don't—"

"It was a *joke!* You were going to laugh. You were."

"For maybe one minute. But swords and blood … I can't even deal with that kind of thing in the movies."

"Movies," said Bart. "I've never had the patience for movies. You'd think we'd just slip into theatres and watch movies whenever we wanted to, but most ghosts don't like them. They're a little too close to what … we are, I guess. The same thing happening over and over again, in a dark room. The world going by outside."

"Yeah. I never liked movies, either," said Alma, and felt herself softening toward Bart again—just a little. But not nearly enough. "I thought I was the only one on the planet who doesn't like movies. But I'm not a ghost, Bart. I'm *alive!* God." She put her head in her hands. *In a dark room*, she thought, and then, *a greater darkness.* Everything seemed too cold, too weirdly tragic, too … closed in. Too *dead*. "Bart, this is way too much for me."

"What is?"

"What we've been doing. Seriously. I'm *alive*, Bart. I'm not … of your world." And as soon as Alma said that, a weight lifted from her that she hadn't known she'd been carrying.

"Alma, please," Bart said again, quietly. He put an arm around her, and it was so cold it made her shoulder hurt. "Perhaps you're right about the duel," he said. "Geoff and I got … out of control. I thought we were done with that nonsense, even in jest. We haven't taken out the swords in decades. Each time we do, it costs us. It's great sport, but there are certainly other ways to … wear ourselves away. To *dissipate*. I can think a very sweet one, especially. One that you might enjoy very much. A proper farewell, if you must have one? I had hoped that you and I…" He turned his gaze on Alma. "Oh, my dear, dear lady. I *had* hoped…"

Alma shivered. The thought of being in his icy arms, of kissing him… Why had that seemed like a good idea, ever? She looked back into his bronze eyes. "I don't think I can do that anymore, Bart."

"Why?"

"It scares me." Alma hadn't realized that until she said it. She didn't want to tell him how cold he suddenly felt … how he really did feel like death. *How did I ever get into this thing?*

"I am very, very tired, Alma," said Bart. The lights flickered, but they didn't go off. And then Bart vanished.

Chapter Twelve

Jessie—still in an unbearably good mood—did breakfast the next morning at Bright Day. Alma was beyond tired. She hadn't slept much. She'd driven to work around eight AM, feeling shuddery and hollowed out. Thank God lunch was just grilled cheese and tomato soup. Jess put the soup together and Alma worked the flattop. And Alma let Jessie do the pots.

"God, look at *you!*" Mary had just shown up for her shift. Alma was in the stockroom, making sure there really was enough linguine for the clam sauce on the supper menu.

"Am I that bad?" said Alma. "What's in the big carton up there?"

"Enough linguine to feed the whole town. Of *course.* You worry too much." Mary grinned. "Alma, you look like you've seen a ghost, nudge-nudge, wink-wink."

Alma rolled her eyes.

A squeal and then a rapturous peal of laughter came from the kitchen. Jan had just arrived.

Fabulous, thought Alma.

"So, your place as soon as I get off work?" he was saying. "I got me a *real* easy meal to cook. Yee-haw!"

"*Yee-haw?*" said Alma. "Those two."

"Ain't love grand?"

"I wouldn't know," Alma said.

Mary dropped her voice. "You wouldn't? You can't be…"

"What?" said Alma.

"Jealous," Mary whispered.

"Of Jess and Jan? Shit, no!"

"'Cause, you know, you've got *Mr. Bartholomew A. Jenkins...*"

"Shhhh..." Alma glanced over her shoulder ... at nothing. *Broad daylight. No one's there.* "Oh, Hell," she said. "Come on outside with me for a minute."

There was a loud clunk just behind them then, where the big cans of honey and maple syrup were. And another, louder one. then a third. The bare light bulb hanging over Alma's head swung wildly back and forth, went off, and flickered back on. Twice.

Mary gasped, but Alma was already picking up the three thirty pound tins from the floor. Mercifully, their lids had stayed on and there was no flood of grade B maple syrup (straight from Vermont). Or of local wildflower honey.

"What's going *on* back in there?" called Jessie.

"Nothing. I shouldn't come to work on no sleep," Alma called back. "Makes me clumsy. Hey, Jan. Your chopped clams are defrosting in the cooler. Mary's back here with me. I'm stealing her for a couple of minutes."

She and Mary walked outside together. It was a cool day and the sun felt good on Alma's face. She pulled off her toque and shook out her hair. They kicked their way through piles of fallen leaves to a swing set, empty with the kids still in their classes. Beyond it, the river shimmered.

"Shit. What just happened?" said Mary. "I was talking about your ghost guy and bam. You think he got pissed off and did that?" She sat down on a swing and Alma took the one beside her.

Alma shrugged. "Nah. Probably his best buddy, Geoff," she said. "I told you, Geoff likes pranks."

"Wow."

"Yeah." The water was mostly green and bronze in the afternoon sun, but silver in places. It was beautiful—and alive. *If you look long enough, you can see every color there is in the Hudson River.* Alma and Mary swung back and forth. "Look, the ghost thing isn't like having a real boyfriend. It never gets to see the light of day. Ghosts do weird things."

Mary nodded. "Of course, there is the having red-hot sex with you part. And the pouring you glasses of wine part. And the calling you m'lady."

"How about the fighting a super bloody fake duel to freak out your ex-husband who just turned up at your place because your *mother* gave him your address part?"

"Whoa. Whoa. Wait a minute. Back up. What kind of soap opera is this? Your mother gave *Stefan* your address?"

"Yeah."

"And so *Bart*…"

"…*and* Geoff were running around stabbing each other with big, long swords and bleeding goo and coughing up… I don't know—ectoplasm or something. To freak out Stefan, you know? They thought it was the funniest thing ever. Stef was drunk on his ass, as per normal. Bart waved a sword at him and he ran away so fast he fell down the stairs, almost. And then Bart and Geoff were like 'Ho, ho, ho! No harm done. We're *ghosts!*' Freaked me the *hell* out."

"I don't know, Alma. I think maybe your mom's the asshole, there."

"Yeah, maybe. Being as Stefan fucking knows where I *live* now. But the whole thing was really, truly gross. It was just … *weird.* Too weird. Like a horror movie except for real."

"Said the girl who told me she had the absolute *best*…"

"Mary, Bart's hands last night were like ice. *Dead* ice. Because ghosts are *dead.* And I'm not. Which may be the most obvious and dumb thing I have ever said in my whole damn life, but there you have it."

"Since you put it that way…" The swings squeaked rhythmically as Mary and Alma glided back and forth.

"So I kind of kicked him out."

"You kicked out a ghost. Don't you need a priest or something for that? Or a séance at least? Did he really leave?"

"I don't know," said Alma.

"Yikes. What do you do if he comes back?"

"I have no idea. I told Cleo yesterday that maybe the whole thing was just a one-nighter—"

"With a ghost. A one-nighter with a ghost," said Mary. "Yeah, she told me."

"Shhhh!"

"Your life! Crazy, crazy, crazy!" said Mary.

"Yeah, I know. Hey. You know Charlie from the Health Department? He's playing fiddle and mandolin at The Cracked Bell open mic tonight. I saw him in town yesterday and he really, really wanted me to come hear him."

"*What?* Now you're blowing off the ghost for Charlie *Sassian*? No! No way!"

"I'm not blowing off a ghost for Charlie Sassian. I'm just blowing off a ghost. Charlie is an old hippie or something. But he's actually kind of charming when he's not busting you for grotty cooler shelves."

"Oh, Alma. Do I *detect*?"

"*No!* But obviously, I need to get out of my apartment, Mary. I mean, you said so once your very own self."

Mary threw back her head and laughed. She pushed back in the swing and rode it into the air, laughing. The sun caught her brown hair and found the gold highlights in it. Alma swung beside her, enjoying the light and the river dazzle … and the thought of an un-complicated evening out. She pumped her legs and closed her eyes and loved the wind puffing out the jacket of her whites.

Then the chain of Mary's swing snapped. "Shit!" said Mary as she landed on her butt in a pile of fallen leaves.

"Shit!" said Alma as she jumped off her swing and rushed over to her. "You okay?"

"I'm fine," Mary said, brushing the dust of her jeans. "I should get inside and get into my whites, and not play on swings meant for school kids. Oh, wow. You don't think that Geoff … or *somebody*…"

Alma shivered, even though the sun on her face was still warm. "Nah," she lied. "He wouldn't do that. I'll call maintenance before I go home. Get it fixed. Good thing that didn't happen with a kid on it."

Chapter Thirteen

When Alma turned the key in her car's ignition after work, nothing happened. She twisted it again, not even a click. But the third time was the charm—except then "I Ran (So Far Away)" by Flock of Seagulls at full volume plus almost blew out her speakers.

I hate that song! Did I even have the radio on going in? She clicked it off. *Geoff!* "You leave me the hell alone, Geoff! I mean it!" she said out loud, signaling for the left turn up her hill.

Maybe it worked. Her apartment was full of very late afternoon sun when she got home, and the place felt peaceful. Alma blasted the remnants of grilled cheese grease off herself in the shower. Hot water and her sweet-smelling shampoo reset her mood, and after she'd blown her blonde curls most of the way dry, it wasn't too hard to tame them again.

She was a little surprised by how much she was looking forward to an evening at The Cracked Bell. No big expectations, no dumb crush on an employee fantasies … and no ghosts! She slipped into a pair of black stirrup leggings and a long, orange tunic. Just the thing for the Thursday before Halloween.

But a greenish glow from behind her lit up the mirror the minute she tilted her head back to put on her eyeliner.

Oh, crap. This time Geoff didn't even say hello. "You're going to break his heart, you know," he said. Alma resisted the urge to turn around and confront him until her eye makeup dried.

"I told you to leave me alone."

"He's *very* upset," said Geoff.

She fanned her eyelids with her fingertips and carefully opened her eyes the rest of the way. Geoff stood next to her in a long blue jacket with many buttons on it smoking a clay pipe.

"You two…" said Alma. "Look, I told Bart I can't even watch gory movies. And you two did a full-on duel reenactment in my apartment and splattered God knows what all over the place."

"Bart cleaned it up," said Geoff. He drew on his pipe and blew a smoke ring.

"That's not the point."

"We scared Stefan away for you."

"True. But still…"

"Now you're going out to meet someone else. You're even … *painting* for him!" Geoff pantomimed putting eyeliner on his own eyes.

"Geoff," said Alma. "You and Bart are going to have to understand that I am *alive*. And you … you two are *dead*."

Geoff snuffed out his pipe. "There's no reason to be rude about it," he said. He put his pipe in a pocket of his jacket, and then he disappeared.

Alma sighed and thought of Bart. Who was he, really? A ghost who could … well, a ghost who knew what to do in bed. But also a man who killed someone in a duel and got himself killed, too. And someone who thought it was funny to keep playacting the duel! That wasn't exactly great boyfriend material.

Alma slipped into a black cashmere coat that had belonged to her grandfather. It was huge on her, but she'd seen women in downtown Manhattan wear men's coats like that with the sleeves rolled up, showing off the lining. She liked the style. Alma had loved her grandfather, and that gave the coat an extra layer of comfort. Besides, her blue bathroom rug jacket clashed with the sweater. *The hell with it*, she thought. *I'm going out!* Her car started right up this time.

She stood outside The Cracked Bell for a minute after she got there, peering through the glass on its tall green door. It was a welcoming place, dimly lit and lined with well-worn booths with leather seats. The servers were taking care of a small crowd, mostly hippies the last decade had forgotten, guys with beards and banjos, and women with serious Little House on the Prairie skirts. Lots of guitars and calico. But no Charlie. Alma pulled the door handle open anyway.

A couple of the bearded guys were setting up wooden folding chairs around a stage at the back of the bar. Charlie was there, tuning his fiddle to one of the pioneer gal's guitars. He had on another long-sleeved tie-dye shirt—and a leather vest! Alma didn't know anyone who dressed like that anymore, but she had to admit the look wasn't too awful on him. The crazy colors in the shirt brought out the copper in his hair. She watched the bartender hand Charlie a sausage roll, which he bit into like he'd never heard of The Department of Health. He washed it down with a few hearty gulps of brown ale.

"Alma!" Charlie brushed pastry crumbs from the sausage roll off his fingertips as he made his way across the room to her. "Hey, you made it!"

"Yeah." They were quiet for a minute, Charlie with a very large smile on his face. Alma smiled, too. She couldn't *not* smile when someone was looking at her that way.

Okay. What do I say to him? "Nice place. I haven't been in here before. Wow, I'd never have thought... I mean, you told me yesterday, but I had no idea you were into this stuff, Charlie! Just look at your, um, tie-dye..." *No, no, no. That was totally the wrong thing. Mentioning the tie-dye was maybe even a bit mean...*

"Ah, the tie-dye. Well, I have a terrible, terrible

thing to admit to you, Alma. I have been known to listen to … The Grateful Dead."

"Yeah, I figured…" Alma remembered Dead Heads from college—smoky dorm rooms, incense, sleepy gatherings with much giggling and rambling guitar music on the stereo. *It actually was kind of cool… Wait a minute, Charlie's saying something…*

"It all was because of Jerry!" he was saying. "Jerry *Garcia*, I mean…"

"I know who *Jerry Garcia* is, Charlie!" Alma's smile was now so big that it was hurting her cheeks.

"Oh, dear. I'm over-explaining again. I do that sometimes. My therapist said I need to… crap, stop talking too much. Um. Thanks for coming!" Charlie was blushing now, and with his pale, freckled face, it was quite dramatic.

"So. About Jerry Garcia…"

"Not everyone knows he plays acoustic music as well as the psychedelic stuff. Like old string-band sounding stuff. I really got into it, so I dusted off my violin from high school and started playing along with the first Old And In The Way album. You said you liked them, right? I guess I got— Well, kind of okay at playing fiddle. You tune a mandolin the same way, so it was easy to jump over onto playing one of them, too. Now old time music is maybe the most important thing in my life."

"Not inspecting kitchens?"

"Shit, no! I mean I want to do a very good job at that because it is my job. To inspect kitchens. It's like doing good for people, too—making sure the food around here is wholesome and stuff. You have to have a job, you know. I mean… I'm babbling, aren't I?"

"No," said Alma, and then she giggled. "Well actually, I lied. You are absolutely babbling. But it's okay. And you do have to have a job." It was cute the way Charlie said "shit." He'd actually looked nervous about it. Kitchen rats usually threw around the worst language possible.

"Here, sit up front with the players! Have you had dinner? I bet you didn't have dinner. Chefs never eat actual food. That's so crazy, isn't it? Do you like fish and chips? The fish and chips here are really good. I'll get you some if you want. And a beer!" He called across the room to the bar. "Hey, Kevin, can I get an order of fish and chips and a nut brown ale for the lovely lady?"

"Thanks," said Alma, but Charlie was already on the way to pick up her pint. He flew back to her table holding it.

"I gotta get this open mic running," he said. "Thanks for coming, Alma. Really. And ... um ... cheers!" He leaned over and pecked her on the cheek just as she was lifting the ale to her lips. It was only a good-friends kiss, but she hadn't expected it. A splash of ale went up her nose and she sneezed. Hard.

"Oh, God. I'm so sorry," said Charlie.

Alma wiped her nose with a napkin and snorted. "It's fine," she said, and it was.

The music turned out to be pretty wonderful, lots of vocal harmonies and tinkly high string notes. A song she didn't know but really liked was called "Sin City," and there was another one she recognized "The Glendale Train." Charlie's fiddle and mandolin playing danced on top of everything. Several times, when he took a solo on mandolin or fiddle, Alma felt Charlie's green eyes on her. When she looked back at him, he winked. Nobody winked at people anymore and Alma decided she liked it. Charlie had also been right about the fish and chips, someone in The Cracked Bell kitchen was an expert on the fry-o-later.

But just before eleven, Alma figured she needed to go. She was opening the Bright Day kitchen in the morning, the night before had been beyond crazy, and she really needed sleep. The second set had just broken up, anyway, and a few of the guitarists were already packing up. Charlie was stepping off the stage when Alma got up and slid her arms back into her coat.

"You're not *going*?" he said.

"Gotta cook breakfast in the AM," she said.

"The kids can't just fix their own? Terribly lazy of them, don't you think?"

"I'm utterly shocked, Charlie. Consider the sanitation violations!"

Charlie laughed. "Guess I'll walk you to your car, then." Charlie held open the pub's big front door for Alma and they walked out together. It was cold. She stuck her hands in her grandfather's huge pockets and remembered something about the original owner of her coat. Her grandpa had been a winking man, too. She felt sad with missing him and happy at the memory at the same time.

That was when she realized how little she was looking forward to going back to her apartment. After the music and the warmth of the pub, the thought of her place made her feel lonely—and more than a little nervous. Suppose Bart showed up all broken-hearted and weird. How do you get an amorous ghost to go away? Worse, there was her ex-husband! *He knows where I live now.* That thought left her shuddering. She and Charlie walked down the sidewalk together, past The Old Fascist.

"I wish you didn't have to go," said Charlie.

"I wish I didn't have to go, too," said Alma, and felt her heart speed up. *Should I tell him?* "My ex-husband showed up the last night, drunk. Freaked me

out. He wasn't supposed to know where I live."

"Whoa," said Charlie, and Alma glanced up at his face. He was frowning. "Is your ex like … *dangerous*?"

"Just crazy," said Alma. "It was an ugly scene." *Way to tell the truth by leaving out all the details.*

"Sounds like," said Charlie.

Alma snuck a hand out of her pocket and took Charlie's arm. "Also," she said, "my place is haunted. For real."

Charlie chuckled, and pulled Alma's hand closer with his elbow. "Tis the season," he said. They were passing a shop window painted with a ghost rising out of a grave and frightening something that looked a little like Godzilla.

"So I've noticed," said Alma.

"No, seriously," said Charlie. "It's the old Celtic holiday of Samhain, not just Halloween. This stuff is ancient. Hang out with Irish fiddle players, you hear the stories. They say that the veil between the dead and the living is really thin at this time of year. Stuff gets all stirred up, you know."

"Trust me, I do," Alma said. *Enough true confessions for tonight.*

"Hey, Alma," said Charlie. "Come back to my place instead. No ex-husbands. No ghosts."

Alma almost said yes instantly, but she just couldn't make the words come out. "I have to be at Bright Day tomorrow at six thirty," she said. "I mean it. I have to *go to sleep!*" They were almost back at her car, now.

"Well, I'm just shocked. What kind of boy do you think I am?" Charlie laughed and shrugged his hair over his shoulders.

"I wouldn't know," said Alma. "What kind of boy are you? Tell me."

Charlie swung around and stood in front of her. "Probably not entirely normal," he said. "Look, you really could sleep at my place if you want. The stuff about your ex sounds bad. I live down on Hentila, by the river. Inherited the house from my uncle. I have the whole place, and there's a spare bedroom. No roommates. I promise, I'll leave you alone. I mean I'll let you sleep. I mean … oh, *shit*."

"Okay," said Alma.

"What? *Really?*"

"Yeah," said Alma, and the tightness that had been riding around inside her stomach ever since the fake duel eased—and then disappeared. "That's your Capri down by River Street, yes? Lead and I'll follow."

"Whoa," said Charlie. "Whoa. I gotta … gotta go get my mando and my fiddle. Um …um, get in your car and turn on the heat so you don't freeze, okay? I don't want you to catch a cold. I really don't." He darted back toward The Cracked Bell.

Chapter Fourteen

Charlie's house was surprisingly cozy for a single guy's place—and clean. *Health Department influence, I guess,* thought Alma as she walked into a tidy living room with heavy, comfortable-looking oak furniture and floor pillows with elaborate geometric patterns on them. There were framed pictures on the walls—not posters. There was even a wildly colorful Indonesian-looking shawl tossed over the back of Charlie's well-worn leather couch.

"This is so … *civilized,*" said Alma.

"Yeah. I can't take all the credit," Charlie said. "My aunt and uncle were the greatest people ever. They died on their way home from Tibet right after I got out of school. Motor scooter crash going to the airport. I used to spend part of every summer here—when they weren't traveling. They never had kids. The rest of the family is downstate. Dad works on Wall Street."

"I'm from Westchester," said Alma.

"Wow. Both of us," said Charlie. "Irvington."

"Briarcliff Manor. My folks work at SUNY Purchase."

"Hah," said Charlie.

"Any siblings?"

"Nope."

"Me, neither," Alma said. "But my mom's really…"

"Intense? Yeah, mine, too," said Charlie. "So is my dad. You want decaf? Another beer? Tea?"

"I have to *sleep,*" said Alma. "Really. I wasn't fooling. I get up at six at the very latest, and I, um, didn't get a lot of rest last night. The thing with my ex, and stuff."

"Six. Yeah, I guess breakfast at the school… I'll

put in headphones if I listen to anything. C'mon upstairs."

Alma followed him up a creaky flight of stairs covered with a worn red and blue rug.

"Here you go," he said, and opened a door to a room with a twin bed covered in a handmade quilt. A dozen tiny origami cranes circled over it—a mobile. There was a framed Hot Tuna concert poster on the wall and a clean white curtain hung in the window. "I used to stay in here when I was a kid," he said. "Let me get you one of my shirts to sleep in."

What single guy lives like this? she wondered. *The place looks like a million cleaning ladies just left.*

Charlie stuck his head back in the door, waving yet another tie-dye. "I'll put out a spare toothbrush and some fresh towels in the bathroom. It's at the end of the hall."

A spare *toothbrush!* "Charlie," said Alma, "Your house is kind of incredible. And you actually keep a spare tooth…"

"Hey. Maybe I actually buy more than one toothbrush at a time. Even though I'm a heterosexual man. My aunt and uncle had great taste. And I like to restore old furniture." He tossed the t-shirt on the bed.

"Wow," said Alma. "I really was gleeped out thinking about going home tonight," she said. "I didn't know how much until I got here. Thanks, Charlie. A lot. I mean it."

"Does that mean you *will* have dinner with me this weekend?" he said, then took a sudden, long-legged step across the room, put his hands on Alma's shoulders, and pecked her cheek again. There was nothing ghostly about his hands on her shoulders and his lips were warm. Charlie raised his bushy red eyebrows and grinned.

Alma's face went hot. She hoped she wasn't

blushing too deeply. "Okay," she said. *Damn, I wanted that kiss. That's crazy. So, do I kiss his cheek, now? No. That would be silly. Or maybe not. He looks kind of wonderful. This house is amazing. Maybe I should ... how did I even end up here?*

He took a step backward, looking into her eyes, and smiled. "So, um, let's be in touch tomorrow. I happen to know where you work and stuff. G'night!" He walked out of the room and closed the door behind him.

Alma slipped out of her clothes and into the t-shirt, which was almost dress-length on her. Wow, the guy used dryer sheets. The shirt actually smelled of lavender. It wasn't even too weird to walk down the hall wearing it to wash her face and use the spare toothbrush. Downstairs, Charlie was locking the front door and humming a song she'd heard him play that night. As Alma walked back to the spare bedroom in her bare feet, she heard Charlie run water in the bathroom, flush the toilet, and close his bedroom door. A radiator hissed somewhere.

Then, the house was quiet. Hentila Avenue had little traffic on it at night. Nothing dramatic or wildly intense was going on. Charlie's house felt like a home, not a ramshackle kitchen-rat apartment. Alma thought about Bart a little after she climbed into bed and pulled the pretty quilt over herself, but in the cozy bedroom it was hard to believe anything like that had ever happened. She slept more soundly than she had in weeks.

Showering the next morning was amazingly un-strange, too. Alma woke up before the alarm she'd set. She caught her breath when she opened the bedroom door to a green glow in the pre-dawn hallway. But it was only a nightlight, not Geoff. Of course, Charlie would have nightlights! The Doctor Bronner's Peppermint soap in the shower was no surprise, either. He was an old hippie, after all. The soap was rough stuff, but it did wake you right up.

Alma put on her grandfather's coat, shut the front door quietly behind her, and backed her car out of the driveway, listening to her radio. There was a new song from Paul McCartney and Michael Jackson, *The Girl Is Mine*. It was a gentle song with sweet lyrics. But she had to admit to herself that she'd liked the live music she'd heard the night before better. *Funny thing about that*. She hoped like crazy that Geoff wouldn't have avenged Bart's broken heart on the bread order, or the flour, or...

She parked her car outside Bright Day's main building in the cold, silent almost-dawn. There was a breeze off the river and a few red maple leaves tumbled onto her windshield. It was too chilly for the OD child care workers to be chatting over cigarettes outside their cottages full of sleeping kids. As for the bread order, everything was as it should be, untouched. Seven dozen assorted bagels in the bakery box inside the door. Three whole wheat Pullmans for PBJ subs later.

And best of all ... no Geoff, thanks be to every bit of luck and goodness in the world! Alma looked nervously around herself as she opened up the kitchen. Benny wasn't there yet to set up.

"Hey," she said out loud. "Thanks for not bugging me this morning, Geoff. Really. I do appreciate it."

No reply.

She walked into an undisturbed stockroom, got some clean whites to change into, and tucked her hair into a toque. Then, Alma put the box of bagels on the counter, took out a serrated knife and a cutting board, and began the job of slicing each one down the middle so she could heat them in the oven for the kids' breakfast.

"Hi, Alma," said Benny, as he walked in. His

hands were in his jean pockets and his voice was quiet.

"How you doing?" she said.

"Not good," said Benny. "Judy says I can't be a BMW for Halloween."

"Oh, dear," said Alma. "I'm sorry. That stinks."

"Yeah."

"So what's your second choice?"

"She says I could be a ghost. She says it would be easy. I don't want to be a ghost."

Shit. Please, don't let this be a cue for something. Please.

But it wasn't. Benny went into the stockroom and got a clean apron.

"Could I mix up the OJ today?" he asked.

"Sure," said Alma. "Wash your hands first. Hey. You could be a monster chef for Halloween. I'll give you a toque—a chef's hat. Judy can to put Frankenstein makeup on you. Would that work?"

"Maybe," said Benny.

"*I* think it would be really cool," said Alma.

"Maybe," he said again. But then he made a changing-gears sound, counting them off as he started to work. Alma didn't stop him. Breakfast went off with no problems.

Then Jessie arrived, full of Halloween plans and laughter. "What? No music?" she said, "It's too quiet in here! We still doing the chili today?"

"Yeah, chili with grated cheese and sour cream. Corn bread. Salad. That ranch dressing I've been making. You want to go downstairs and get a bunch of big onions and bell peppers?"

Jessie sorted through the box of cassettes next to the kitchen's boom box. "First thing's first. Tunes. Nick Lowe? The Jam?"

"That Hot Tuna tape still in there?"

"Hot *Tuna?* The one Max left behind when he split? Really?"

"Yeah," said Alma, and smiled. "Crank it."

Chapter Fifteen

"Oh, shit," said Jessie. She'd just finished scouring out the chili pot. "Health Department! I thought they were done with us? What the hell is Sassian after *now*?" She pointed out the kitchen window at Charlie's battered Capri.

Alma looked up from the counter where she'd been writing out the weekend bread order. She beamed and then danced over to the sinks, grabbed the steel scrubber from Jessie's hand, and stashed it inside the dish machine. Better safe than sorry, after all. "Relax, Jessie. It'll be fine," she said. "They're not after us. I went out to hear Charlie play music last night—"

Jessie whooped. "Whoa! That's why you're all smiley! You went out with Charlie Sassian! Ha!"

"I went out to *hear* Charlie Sassian. He plays string band music. Country rock. Like that."

"Charlie *Sassian?*"

"Knock, knock." Charlie stuck his head in the kitchen door. He had on his Health Department duds— the ugly polo shirt and chinos—and his hair was back in its workday ponytail. But he had a bouquet of chrysanthemums in his hand instead of a clipboard.

"Hey," said Alma.

"I brought you these," he said. "They're only from the grocery store, but I thought … you know. I mean, there's no real reason you couldn't have them in here. No *regulation*, I mean. Against flowers in a vase. Because I wanted to…"

Jessie caught Alma's eye from across the kitchen and mouthed "No way!"

Alma took the flowers. "You brought me fleur! Thank you! Shall we step outside?" She shot a warning glance at Jessie, and then followed Charlie out to the swing set and the view of the river, sticking her nose in the flowers as they walked. She'd always loved the smell of chrysanthemums, sharp and bracing instead of sugary-sweet. "*Pretty* fleur," she said.

"I like the color. Gold, like your hair. But I mean, they're only from the grocery. I mean, they're all wrapped up in plastic. I mean, oh, dungballs, I can't do this stuff. I—"

"*Dungballs?*" Alma laughed. "They're lovely. I figured you'd just call. It's good to see you, though."

Charlie looked serious. "I figured you'd be getting off work around now," he said. "I thought about your ex-husband … and you going back to your apartment alone. I got worried."

Oh, my. Alma looked down into the flowers again so Charlie wouldn't see her smiling so hard. "Stefan's a harmless drunk," she said. "I hate it that he knows where I live, but I don't think…" She shivered a little. The sun was bright, but the wind hadn't let up. November was clearly coming.

"I just had a bad feeling," Charlie said. "Like a premonition or something. Let me walk into your place with you. Please?"

"Oh, *God*. A *premonition*," Alma said—and immediately regretted it. "Oh, crap. I didn't mean to sound sarcastic and stuff. My mom thinks she's *psychic*. I get these phone calls. But … you know … Charlie, it's complicated. *Really* complicated. As in, you have no idea."

Charlie nodded. "Complicated is fine with me. I'll wait 'till you get out of your whites. Do you have much more to do?"

"No," said Alma. "And I think these flowers are about to decorate my place, not the Bright Day kitchen. Lemme see. I have to call the bakery, order is in for the veg and meat. Mary has got to be on her way in … Ten minutes."

In the bathroom next to the stockroom, she took time to reapply her eyeliner and fluff her hair.

Suppose Charlie is right. Suppose Stefan got in, somehow—maybe talked the landlord into letting him up. Nah. Peter wouldn't fall for that—or would he? And what about Bart? But Bart wouldn't show up now, in the afternoon...

Alma started her Valiant. She beeped at Charlie in his Capri and he followed her up the hill to her apartment. Enough leaves were down now so that the sun was bright on her living room walls as they walked in. The light flickered a little with the shadows of moving branches.

"Okay. Indulge me," said Charlie. He walked through the place with Alma behind him. Out into the kitchen. Down the hall. Through her bedroom.

"I guess I should check this, too," said Alma, and opened her closet, which was full of nothing but clothing. "Nope. No ex-husband in there."

"I hope you don't think I'm being ridiculous. Or that I just wanted to … you know … get myself let into your place or something. I mean, I don't operate like that. I mean…" Charlie stood next to Alma's bed and looked into her eyes and then at his feet.

Alma smiled. "I don't. Think you're ridiculous, that is."

"Because I say what I mean. Too much of it sometimes. You still want to have dinner with me, right? Like tonight? Is that crazy? We said this weekend. It's officially the weekend now, right? Friday. But you must have plans. I mean, you might even have a *boyfriend* or something, I guess. You might…"

Bart. But that was only a one-nighter. Maybe I

really did manage to break up with him... His touch had been so cold the last time she'd seen him. *Cold as the grave*, she thought, and felt chilled just thinking it.

"Are you okay?" said Charlie. "You look really serious."

"I look that way, sometimes," said Alma. "I'm okay. Let me get these mums into some water." Charlie followed her into the kitchen, and she found an old milk bottle that had been in the apartment when she first rented it. She took out her chef's knife to trim off the bottom of the flowers' stems.

"Yikes," said Charlie. "A gorgeous woman with a *great big knife*."

Alma laughed. Was that as good as being called ravishing? She felt another pang of guilt about Bart. "I'd love to have dinner with you tonight, Charlie."

"You liked my house. How about we eat there? Do you like sea scallops?" asked Charlie. "Joe at Columbia Seafood had some this week. I'm no chef, but I have learned a little from hanging out in kitchens. I sear them and then I can do that butter sauce thing..." He was blushing again.

"Seared sea scallops! You're not afraid that..."

"Not for two adults our age in reasonably good health, in a non-institutional setting. It's actually quite different for... Oh, shut up, me." Blushing, Charlie shook his head, but smiled. "So, seven o'clock? I gotta go close up things back at the department."

Alma found herself smiling too hard again and then she found herself very conscious of what she was wearing—yesterday's clothes. "Sounds good. I really do need to change and shower. Should I bring wine?" She walked him to the door, and noticed her answering machine was flashing. *My mother again. Gotta be.*

"Yeah," said Charlie. "So, I guess I'll just ... like

… go zip out and buy us some scallops and um, that." He picked up Alma's right hand and held its palm to his lips. The sweetness of the gesture startled her.

"Thanks for coming up." Alma opened her arms and they fell into a blind, clumsy hug. Alma could feel a trace of his belly against her, the roughness of his awful tweed jacket—and smell a hint of Doctor Bronner's Peppermint soap. Charlie kissed her on the top of the head then. The contact was comforting, but it also made her a little light-headed. She felt enveloped in something she couldn't identify. Was it safety? Then why did she feel so … fizzy?

"So…" she said.

"Yeah," said Charlie again, and gave her another squeeze. "I'm going now. See you in a couple of hours."

Alma's cheeks ached from smiling so much by now. "Bye," she said, and watched Charlie walk down the stairs.

She closed her apartment door and listened to her messages. Three of them, all in her father's deep, deliberate voice. All the same. "Alma, please call home right away. We're both all right, but your mother is too upset to come to the phone right now. We need to speak."

Her stomach knotted instantly and she tapped out her parents' number with shaky hands. *This is bad. This has got to be bad. He said they're all right… Something terrible happened. Did they crash the car?*

Her father picked up the phone. "Professor Kobel," he said, as he always did, whether he was at work or home. You couldn't figure anything out from his voice.

"Dad?" said Alma. "I'm sorry. I was out. What happened?"

"No. It's not us. It's Stefan," he said, and exhaled

slowly. "He appears to have been… Oh, this is difficult, Alma. Stefan took a fall down the stairs in his loft sometime last night." Alma remembered the sleeping arrangements in the place she'd shared with her ex. The bed was up a flight of steel steps. Steep and noisy to walk on, the stairs moved under you just a bit, which was a real pain when you had to get up to use the bathroom.

"Stefan showed up *here* for a while, Dad. On Wednesday. He said Mom told him where I—"

"I know. She really shouldn't have done that."

"He's in the hospital?"

"This is going to be a nasty shock for you, I'm afraid. He's dead, Alma. Broken neck. Probably cracked his skull, too. His brother, Adrian … found him. Your mother had talked to Stefan sometime Thursday afternoon. She and I have reason to believe that he was a bit…"

"Drunk," said Alma. "He was *really* drunk when I saw him. It was like he was on one of his … you know. Oh, my God." She stared out her living room window at the afternoon sun dipping into the remaining yellow leaves. She felt blank, not grieved. She'd never even really missed Stefan when she moved out. There had been a period of feeling lost, and then there was the life she had now. *He was my husband for eight years. Shouldn't I at least need to cry?* But she actually felt … relieved. And then guilty for feeling that way.

"…the executrix," her father was saying. "His lawyer's appalled, but there you have it. You must know how your mother felt about Stefan. It seems it was mutual."

Alma sighed. "That's insane. Mom's the executrix of his *will*?"

"Apparently so. We'll know more soon. The wake is tomorrow, and the funeral is Monday. Adrian didn't want a fuss, and he's all the family Stefan had. But Stefan also had ... students, you know, and he *was* well-regarded. *The New York Times* was about to run an article on him—did your mom tell you? I don't know what you should attend, Alma. I don't know that you *want* to attend. Your mother and Adrian set everything up. Are you on any kind of good terms with Adrian?"

Stefan's parents were both long dead. The last time Alma had seen Adrian was at an art opening shortly before the separation. He'd ignored her except for hellos and goodbyes. That was what he usually did.

"I have no idea," said Alma. "How come Stefan sicced an attack lawyer on me and my mother is executrix of his will?"

"A mystery," said her father.

"Wow," said Alma. "Wow."

"Are you very upset, dear?"

"God, Dad. It's not like Stefan and I—"

"I know, I know. Do me a favor. Call your mother tomorrow. She took a pill. She's sleeping now."

"Okay."

"Are you my own girl?" That's what her father always said to her at the end of phone conversations— that is, when he actually called her, which was only a few times a year—unless something dreadful happened and her mother had taken a pill. But Alma teared up anyway. For the little she knew of her father, not for Stefan.

"Yeah, Dad. I'm your own girl. Guess ... I'll see you at the funeral. I can't do the wake."

I must be some kind of monster. Alma then she thought about Bart again. *I'm cruel to the living—and the dead. Occasionally even at the same time!*

Chapter Sixteen

Alma showered and changed into a fresh pair of jeans—high-waisted ones, that nipped in nicely and showed off her figure. After putting on her makeup very carefully, she found her very favorite shirt, the one she'd never worn to work. The big cabbage rose print, muted rose and green, with bat-wing sleeves looked fabulous on her. It was still only a little after five, but it was getting pretty dark—dark *enough*, anyway. And no Bart. Or maybe he really did understand the affair was over. That a one-nighter was a one-nighter.

She'd never felt quite so nervous in her own apartment. She thought about putting on a record and then couldn't decide what she wanted to hear. She sat down on her couch, picked up the Mary Stewart book, and put it down again. And got back up.

"Bart," she said out loud, just in case. "I'm going to go out. I'm sorry. I…"

There was no response. *Maybe he really has packed up and left. Do ghosts do that? And suppose I end up spending another night at Charlie's?* Should she discreetly pack a change of clothing? Was a dinner invite just a dinner invite or … no, that hug had felt like more than a dinner invite.

What her father had just told her on the telephone crashed back down on her then. *Here I am, just having heard that the man I was married to has died and I'm worried about a change of clothes because I'm about to have … a one-nighter?* No, if she stayed at Charlie's, Alma had a strong feeling it would not be just a one-nighter. Unless, of course, she decided to break *his* heart, too.

What is it with me?

That was when she felt a cold draft through the damp hair at the back of her neck. She turned around to see Bart. He had his long dark jacket on over his white shirt. His face was luminous—and grim.

"Lady," he said. He put his hands on her shoulders, pulling her toward him. It felt like falling into a pool of icy slush.

Alma's stomach turned over. "No, Bart," she said. "Please, don't." It was hard to break from his grasp—and not just because Alma didn't want to. Something terrifying had glued her to him, and she hated it.

"Alma," he said, and she managed to squirm out of his grasp.

"I have to go out, Bart," said Alma, trying to make her voice sound as confident as it did when she was talking to the guy from Sexton Foods for canned tomatoes, or the butcher from Hudson Market. But she was shaking—was it from cold or nerves? Maybe both. Her apartment suddenly felt like the walk-in cooler at Bright Day. Why weren't her words coming out of her mouth in white clouds?

"I…" Bart put his face in his hands for a moment. When he dropped his arms he looked intensely into her eyes. "I wanted to do what Tace did, Alma. I wanted to float away to wherever the next place is, even if it's endless night. No moon or stars." He stepped toward Alma and opened his arms to her. "Dear lady, I wanted to do that by making love to you." He sighed. "But I feared that I'd take you with me if I did."

"Take me with you? But I'm alive! I'm not like you! I'm not… It wouldn't have *killed* me, would it?" The air had gotten so cold in the room that Alma's toes were numb inside their ankle boots.

"I don't know, my dear lady," said Bart. "The

next place is a mystery. Perhaps it would have been … a *marriage*, of sorts…"

Alma didn't know whether she was more frightened—or more angry. "Bart, you have to go right now. You can't stay here, and you can never, ever…"

"I understand that," he said.

They stood silently facing each other. "And it was his *own* damn fault, you know. He brought it on himself."

"Who?"

"Stefan," said Bart, and Alma drew her breath in through her teeth.

"What do you know about Stefan?" She'd thought the very same thing, though, that Stefan's death had been his own fault. That he'd been very drunk, had been drinking for days, had gotten out of bed and fallen. That he'd been out of control and paid the price. In an brutal way, it was a mercy. At least he hadn't killed someone in a car crash on his way home from her apartment. He easily could have. Stefan had always been careless that way. He was also an alarmingly bad driver, even sober.

"What I know is that he shan't bother you ever again," Bart said. "Ever. I promise. I will leave, m'lady. But I will watch … always." He bowed deeply to her.

Alma's thoughts were racing, now. *What if Bart pushed Stefan somehow? Or one of his ghost friends did. Or…* Her eyes began to blur with tears. She had no love left for her ex-husband, but that thought was simply too horrible. "Bart. *You* weren't the one who…"

"Pushed him down the stairs? I certainly would have. With the greatest of pleasure. I despised the man."

"Oh my God, Bart, no. No! I've got to get out of here. I've got to—"

"Don't go." Bart said. "Don't leave me! Please!

Not yet! He fell! That's all, even if he … deserved it. I had nothing to do with it. Nothing."

"*Nobody* deserves it," said Alma. She blinked back her tears. She wondered about something else: suppose Stefan had joined Bart's number! That was something she'd have laughed at a few weeks ago, a plot to a silly movie. "Bart … you don't know where Stefan … *ended up*, do you?" She wrapped her arms around herself and shivered.

"No," said Bart. "Sudden departures like his … of course, there is always a chance. He may have left this sphere utterly. I've known many souls who have. But you have my word as a gentleman. I shall protect you— always. I shall make it my business that you are *never* bothered… Nothing will ever, ever hurt you, Alma. I swear!"

Alma felt sick. *He's lying. He could have killed me. He wanted to kill Stefan.* "No!" she said. "None of this is your business. You and I can't be involved in any way, Bart!"

"Alma!" said Bart. "My lady. Goodbye, my sweetest dove. I don't know how I shall bear it." He grew more and more transparent, and then he disappeared. The lights flickered for a moment—but they stayed on.

It was now fully dark outside. Cars with their headlights on drove up Alma's hill and passed her house. The air in her apartment was suddenly warmer. She heard the radiator in her bedroom ticking. Her landlord was cooking dinner downstairs—cabbagey-smelling something—not too appetizing, but decidedly unghostly. She was still shaking. She wanted to go to Charlie's. It shocked her how much she wanted to go to Charlie's. Twenty 'till six. *Calm down*, she told herself. *Calm down. You have to drive.*

I said I'd bring wine. The store that had the best

prices was a little out of town, near an outlet mall. She could treat herself to a little something in the shop next to it, the one that had sexy underwear. Alma had mostly been a cotton-panties-from-the-bargain-bin girl, but some lace might be just the thing tonight. Then she'd pick up the wine—she decided she'd get a bottle of good champagne and reclaim the stuff from her awful memory of the night she left Stefan.

Bart's gone. Maybe he's gone for good.

Chapter Seventeen

Alma pulled into Charlie's driveway with a bottle of cold Moët & Chandon and a big bag of some very lacy underthings. Plus a really nice, long black nightgown that was just slightly see-through. The champagne had been a splurge, but the lingerie had been so marked down it hardly felt extravagant. The shopping trip had been just what she needed to steady her nerves. She'd even gone back into the dressing room and changed into some of laciest stuff she'd chosen after she paid for it. The saleslady had giggled with her when Alma admitted she was on her way to a hot date.

Alma stuffed the nightgown into her pocketbook and turned off her headlights. Good thing she carried a serious tote bag. It also contained another pair of jeans, a change of underwear, and her second favorite shirt—the purple and grey striped one. She took a minute to breathe. She thought of Bart's pale face and felt guilty— until she remembered that he seemed perfectly willing to risk her life along with whatever existence he had of his own. She remembered how she always used to wake up when Stefan got up at night to use the bathroom, the way the mattress bounced as he stumbled to his feet. She imagined him getting up for the last time... *Oh, God*, she thought again.

Almost every window of Charlie's house was lit. The place looked cheery, almost festive. Charlie threw the door open the moment Alma put her foot on the bottom step of his front porch. He was wearing a dark blue shirt with a batik print on it, button-down, tails out, and a pair of well-washed Levis. His long red hair flowed over his shoulders. Behind him, a sweet-smelling wood fire burned in the living room's stone fireplace.

"Hey," said Alma as she walked in the door.

"Hey." Charlie closed the door behind her and swept her into another bear hug.

"Nice shirt," said Alma.

"My favorite. It was my uncle's. From Bali," he said. "It's so good to see you again, Alma."

"Likewise," said Alma. Her arms were pinned down by his. The bottle of champagne was icy against her thigh. "I brought some nice—"

But then they were kissing. Charlie's mouth was warm, and he massaged Alma's back with strong fingers, pulling her close. His cheeks were smooth of stubble, and soft. For a few moments, the sweetness of the kiss blew everything else that had happened that day away. When Alma finally opened her eyes, he was gazing at her intently.

"Ah, man." He exhaled a hollow whistle. "Phew!"

"Yeah," said Alma. "Um. Want champagne?"

Charlie laughed. "That's right. I did invite you for dinner, I believe. And you do seem to have brought us some. C'mon out to the kitchen. I made curried rice. I've got the scallops and I made a salad … and there's a tiny chocolate cake from Pierre Dumont's."

"Dumont's? Is that the new…" But then they were kissing again. This time, Alma managed to put the bottle of Chandon down first. She leaned into every bit of Charlie. His slightly round belly (actually kind of sweet, she'd decided), his belt buckle, his long legs. She put her arms around his neck and played with his hair. The strands were a little coarse to the touch, and there certainly was a lot of it. His tongue was more urgent this time. She felt his cock come alive as he pressed his hips into hers.

"Mmmmm," someone said. *Oh. That's me.* Every nerve inside of her was buzzing, but she was completely relaxed. Her new panties were a bit scratchy with all their starched black lace—and now just a wee bit moist. But there was no need to rush things.

They were standing in door of the kitchen when they parted. Charlie got two engraved crystal champagne flutes off a high shelf, carefully washed them out in the sink, and dried them with a white kitchen towel. He undid the champagne bottle's wire cage and used the towel to grab the cork. The bottle opened with a gentle pop, as if he'd been working as a sommelier for his whole life.

"Ha. Nice job," said Alma. "Most guys—"

"Are stupid and waste delicious champagne," he said. "You got the good stuff. Cheers! Here's to wild-haired blonde goddesses! Or to this one, anyway." He brought his glass to hers. They sipped. And sipped again.

"Living room?" said Charlie.

"Sure," said Alma. They walked back in together, and settled next to each other on the couch. Alma slipped out of her ankle boots and slid her stocking feet underneath her. The fire snapped and danced, and they stared into it for a few minutes. *Bart*, Alma thought, and felt queasy. *Bart is gone. And I'm in a place of nothing but life and warmth.*

Charlie threw his head back and laughed.

"What's funny?"

"Nothing's funny. I just... I mean ... um ... that was happiness," he said.

"Yeah," said Alma. *How about ... Stefan*, said something inside her. *Stefan's dead. You can't be happy now. You aren't allowed...*

Charlie put down his champagne on the coffee table and put his hands on Alma's cheeks. "Let me just look at you," he said. "Wow. The first time I inspected the Bright Day kitchen ... I couldn't even see your hair under that toque, but I could barely stand to look at you because you were so lovely. Maybe I can deal with it now. Deal with looking at you, I mean."

Alma smiled. "Flattery."

"No," said Charlie. "Reality. You."

He's so incredibly ... solid. Alma looked at the tall, smiling man beside her, and her dark thoughts seemed like a storm in another country. *A nice guy. I thought nice guys weren't supposed to make you feel like this.* Her new panties really were rather uncomfortable. Weren't sexy panties supposed to be *good* for this kind of thing? Apparently not.

She took another sip of her wine and spoke the next thing she thought. "I think it's possible that you are amazing, Charlie."

"Possible?"

"More than that. I also think that we're about to..."

"Oh, *yeah.*" Charlie wrapped his arms around her, pulled her into his lap, and kissed her again, slowly and softly, until they were both out of breath. Then he ran his fingers over her left breast.

"I like that," she said.

"So do I," Charlie said. "And I know a secret. You *hid* something from me right here. Something ... made of stainless steel." He drew out the word *steel* and ran a finger over her breast again, circling around it.

Alma snorted and sat up straight. "No *way!* You saw the scrubber!"

"I'll never admit I was looking down your shirt during an ... *inspection.*"

They kissed again, and then Alma pulled away. *I was just trying to keep my job.* She felt her cheeks go hot, and opened her mouth to say something she couldn't quite find words for when it dawned on her. *He was on my side the whole time.* She smiled. It was okay. It was really okay. *My face has to be super red.*

"*Yes?*" said Charlie. He stroked her breast again. "Of course, a steel scrubber is the only way to get a really dirty pot clean. It was a really *dirty* pot. Dirty, dirty, dirty!"

Alma laughed hard. It was a huge relief to laugh like that. She was burning to run upstairs with this man, and in no rush whatsoever for it to happen any sooner than it did. It was too good just being where she was. "I love this, Charlie."

"Me, too," said Charlie. "I want to feed you … *first*. I really want to feed you. Let's…"

"Okay," said Alma, and thought of Stefan again. *I could tell Charlie about Stefan—or not.* She didn't want to ruin what felt like the loveliest evening she'd had in years. There was the matter of Bart, too but she couldn't even think about how she'd work that into the conversation. *He's gone,* she told herself again.

Charlie stood in front of her. "Up, you glorious thing," he said. "Up!" She took his hands and let him pull her to her feet. "I am about to sear some scallops. And then…"

Chapter Eighteen

Alma and Charlie stood beside each other in the kitchen, rinsing their dinner plates. *Like a married couple.* Except not in her marriage. Stefan hadn't washed a dish in eight years. At his famous dinner parties, the laughter and conversation had always gone on while Alma silently whisked everything out to the sink.

Is this weird? Aren't we supposed to be tearing each other's clothes off about now instead of cleaning up, catching each other's eyes, and grinning like fiends? Maybe I shouldn't have told him about Stefan. But it would have been too weird not to. She licked her cake fork, and then rinsed it and put it next to Charlie's in the dish washer.

Charlie hung a sauce pot on the rack over his stove—a reconditioned restaurant model, an old Garland, Alma had noted with envy. Then he dried his hands on a dish towel and put his arms around her. She buried her face in his chest.

"So your dad called you like a couple of hours ago?"

"Yup."

"But you came over here anyway."

"Yup."

"I'm glad," Charlie said. "It's good that you're here."

Alma pulled away and closed the door on the dishwasher. "God, I didn't want him to *die,* Charlie. But it's almost a relief, and that is so, so weird. Then there's the weirdness with my mom. Executrix."

"I know. I can't get my head around that part."

"*You* can't?" said Alma. "I keep feeling like I should be in mourning. I'm not in mourning."

"He was a drunk. He took you for granted," said Charlie.

"He was. He did."

"He cheated on you and you left him. And he made the divorce super expensive for you. Hard to mourn someone who does that."

"Yeah," said Alma.

"You're allowed to feel the way you feel," Charlie said and kissed Alma, deeply. He ran his hands down her back and pulled her close to him, cupping the curve of her bottom. The ripples of heat Alma had felt before supper washed back into her. She stood on her toes and felt Charlie's cock stiffen beneath his jeans again and press into her belly as he pulled her to him more tightly.

"I guess we haven't managed to talk ourselves out of..."

"No!" said Alma. She looked up into his green eyes. "Oh, God, no."

He grinned—and began to unbutton her shirt.

Charlie," said Alma. "I really want to do this upstairs. I want to be in your bed."

"*Oh yeah?*" He put an arm behind her knees and under her arms, picking her up. And wobbled toward the steps with her.

Alma's scratchy lace underpants slid directly into her crotch. "Yow!"

That stopped Charlie in mid-wobble. "Are you okay?"

She giggled. "Stupid underpants," she said. "This is all very romantic but I am not so light. Put me down. You're going to hurt yourself."

"You happen to be *luscious*. But, okay." Charlie gently set her down, took her hand and darted up the stairs ahead of her. He dropped his hold and ran into his bedroom. "Ta-dah!" he sang, ripping the duvet off his bed. Then he picked Alma up again, and tossed her onto it.

"Let's just *see* about those stupid underpants," he said. But he unbuttoned her blouse the rest of the way first. "Hello! What have we here? Black lace and a scarlet bow!"

"Brand new! And the stupid underpants match."

"All for *me?*" Charlie pressed the tips of his fingers together.

"I don't think they'd *fit* you," she said, but Charlie's hands were already behind her, feeling for hooks. "Oh, the clasp. It's in front. The saleslady said…"

"Bingo!" The bra flew across the room and then Charlie went at work on her jeans. And his own. And his batik shirt. All went airborne. For a moment, he stood in front of her—beaming, naked, pale, slightly round-bellied, and quite substantially erect.

He lay down beside her. Alma ran her fingers over his body, feeling his skin and his shoulders, legs and cock. When Charlie pulled her face to his again, his heat shot straight to her crotch and smoldered there. *Charlie is not a perfect specimen. Just perfectly kind.*

That was the weirdest part. Even after every crazy thing that had happened in the past few days, she was wildly, hugely happy. And yet her underpants were still trying to slice her in two. She reached down to free herself, but Charlie got there first.

"Stupid, stupid underpants," he said, and they flew, too. Charlie and Alma lay face to face for a few minutes, arms around each other. Alma took his cock in her hand and stroked it, feeling it grow in her hand. He spiraled his tongue around her breasts until he got to each of her nipples, and sucked. A sweet, sharp ache started as he added more pressure. He put a hand between her legs and stroked her pussy, then easily slid a finger into her vagina.

"Mmmm," said Alma. "Charlie, that is so good."

"It is." Gently removing his finger, Charlie ran his tongue over her stomach and back up to her breasts again. He kissed the space above her heart, rolled to his side, and propped himself up on his elbow. The grin on his face tempted her to have a little fun of her own. She pushed him on his back and ran her own tongue down his chest to his belly before taking his cock in her mouth. He groaned as she sucked until she tasted salt at its tip. He really was quite big, now. now.

"Oh, Alma," he said. "*Oooh.* Oh, wait. Wait." She heard something crinkle, looked up, and saw him wiggling a silver condom package between two fingers. He slipped his cock out of her mouth. "Check *this* out," he said, and ripped the package open with his teeth. "Behold the *savage!*" He tossed the wrapper across the room and made a snarling sound.

He bent forward to roll the condom over his cock, and then attempted to shake his long mane back over his shoulders. Red hair flew everywhere, including Alma's face. She looped some of it behind his ears. He looked ridiculous. And wonderful.

Charlie snarled again. But then he stopped. "Am I rushing you?" he said in a very un-savage voice. "I wouldn't want to…"

"Good God, *no!*" said Alma. "Please! Rush me! Rush me lots!"

"Excellent," said Charlie, sliding down her body and putting his head between her legs. "Oh, my," he said, and flicked the tip of his tongue over her clit.

More heat flowed through her, ripples, then waves of it, large waves. Charlie lapped and Alma giggled—until she felt like she was flying, like she was on a swing and just about to jump off. "I want you now, Charlie."

Charlie pulled himself back up and looked deeply into her eyes as he slowly entered her.

She gasped.

"I didn't hurt you?"

"Oh. *Oh*. Not at all." That wasn't exactly true. Charlie took some getting used to. Alma was as full as she'd ever been—more so, much more so. She looked back into his eyes, and felt him begin to move inside her.

"Alma. Oh, *God*," Charlie said. "No—Oh, *Science!*" He laughed, and thrust into her again and again. Fire ignited in her.

Then his mouth was over hers. Alma closed her eyes, and they breathed together. She loved the weight of him on her, how incredibly thick his cock was. He pushed, and she pushed back. More fire circled in the depths of her. He wrapped his arms around her and kissed her, more deeply. She felt herself just beginning to come, and stayed that way for what seemed like hours as they moved more slowly together.

Charlie squeezed her closer. "Open your eyes," he said.

When she did, Charlie was watching her intently. "I can see ... *into* you," he said, as he pushed into her, picking up speed. He moaned and she felt his cock throb inside her. She was throbbing, too—all over, inside and out, in her pussy, up her spine. He thrust into her again and she came more intensely. She felt herself shouting something but she didn't know what it was. Another hot wave came, and another. Finally, Charlie lay quietly on top of her, and kissed her again. He pulled out of her carefully, and turned away for a moment.

"Wow," he said. "Let me ... um ... dispose of this latex necessity."

"I didn't tell you that I have an IUD. I'm preggers-proof. You needn't have…"

Charlie pulled the duvet off the floor, tossed it back over her, and got in back in bed beside her. "Health department employee. I get to hear some truly awful stuff. Safety first, I guess. It didn't make you feel…"

"Course not," said Alma.

Charlie put his arms around her and pulled her close again. "That was just so … easy," he said. "Ah, no. That came out wrong. I mean—I didn't mean to say *you* were. Oh, poop. Ack. Did I just put my foot in it again?"

Alma smiled. "It *was* easy. I think maybe it's supposed to be like that."

"Alma," said Charlie, stroking her hair. "Where'd you get a head of hair like this?"

"Mom's Irish," she said. "Maybe from her side of things. What about yours?"

"We're Hudson Valley mutts—Dutch, English, Irish … who knows? The whole family is red-headed. I should run downstairs and make sure the fire's okay for me to leave it overnight. You're going to sleep over and hang out lots and lots tomorrow, aren't you?"

Alma stretched and smiled. "Maybe I'll even cook for you."

"Cook me *dinner!* And then…"

"Dinner? Wow. Okay, if you can stand that much of me."

"If!" Charlie swung his legs over the edge of the bed and pulled his jeans on. "Be right back. Want your … um … nightgown from last night?"

Alma considered the slinky black number in her pocketbook—and then the itchy black lace undies.

"I'd *love* my nightgown from last night," she said. He trotted down the hall and came back with the shirt. Alma slipped the tie-dye over her head, and got up to use the spare toothbrush. Charlie was sitting in bed tuning his mandolin as she slid back under the duvet next to him. He was humming *Oh, Shenandoah*—and picking a harmony against the tune—as she slipped into sleep, curled up beside him.

Chapter Nineteen

Alma slept hard through most of the night, waking up around dawn to peek between the curtains on Charlie's bedroom window. A pink and golden sunrise was lighting up the clouds on the river's other bank and the water glistened with it. Charlie was asleep on his stomach, the mandolin on the floor by his side of the bed. She stood in front of the window for a few minutes, taking it all in. Stefan's death and the queasiness she felt when she let herself think about Bart seemed like something from another lifetime.

When she got back in bed next to Charlie, he woke up halfway and flung an arm over her.

The next time Alma woke, she heard a key in the lock downstairs and jumped. She was alone in bed—and she smelled coffee.

"Alma?" called Charlie. "You were out cold. I ran to Peggy's for jelly doughnuts."

"Peggy's jelly doughnuts?" said Alma. "You are evil. They're addictive."

"Breakfast of champions. One is too many and a hundred is not enough," Charlie said. "So I got four. I figured if I got a dozen…"

"We'd eat them all," said Alma. "*I'd* eat them all."

"Stay put," said Charlie, and a few minutes later, brought in a rattan tray with two big mugs of coffee and a plate of doughnuts. He was wearing a pair of grey sweatpants and a SUNY Oswego sweatshirt. "You slept well, I guess."

"This is a good house for sleeping," said Alma. "Also, you, um—got me nice and relaxed. That was kind of spectacular."

"Oh, *yeah.*" Charlie turned so red his freckles

almost disappeared. "It was." After opening the curtains so they could sit up and look at the river, he set the tray of doughnuts and coffee down at the bottom of the bed. He picked up a jelly doughnut and bit into it. Raspberry jelly squirted out its other end. A thumb-sized red blob dribbled down his chin and landed on his sweatshirt.

"*Very* nice," said Alma.

"Mmmfff!" said Charlie, his mouth full of doughnut. He swallowed and then laughed. "I can't believe I forgot napkins!"

"I'll go get 'em," Alma said. "*You* stay put this time." The phone rang as she ran back upstairs.

"My mom," said Charlie. "Saturday morning at ten. Like a finely-calibrated Swiss watch. I could let it go to machine…"

"Nah. Talk to Mom," said Alma, and took her coffee to the window. How great it was to be this close to the water. The water's sparkle danced on Charlie's white walls as he chatted with his mother about his job.

"I sure did," he was saying. "Yeah, I think they got rid of the rats. Lovely people, but *I* wouldn't eat that kielbasa! They tried to give me one."

Fabulous. Bet that's where my landlord gets 'em! Oh, well, I'm still alive.

Still alive… Alma neatly pushed Bart out of her thoughts, then. But it wasn't so easy to forget who else wasn't. Stefan. *Why don't I feel worse about that than I do?*

Charlie pinched the phone's receiver between his shoulder and his ear, held up his right hand and made a blah-blah-blah gesture. "Yeah, yeah. Okay, I will," he said.

Alma wondered for a moment if he was going to say anything to his mom about her. *Bet he won't. We're still in one-nighter territory, officially anyway.* But unofficially? She smiled at Charlie and he smiled back as he gobbled his second doughnut, listened and nodded. This did *not* feel like a one-nighter. Alma's first date with her Stefan had, though. She remembered crawling back into her dorm at noon with a hangover.

"Yeah, I should go. Got a lot of paperwork this weekend," said Charlie. "Love you, too, Mom. Oh—I had a great date last night. Nuh-*uh*. No, I'm not saying anything else. No, no, and nope." He laughed and winked at Alma.

Wow. Now she actually felt nervous as he hung up the phone. "Do you really have lots of work to do?"

"I don't have *any* work to do," said Charlie. "But I did have a great date last night."

She sat down next to him on the bed and he looked into her eyes, and kissed her. He tasted like coffee and jelly doughnuts, and she laughed and opened her arms. Her breasts were loose under his old T-shirt, and the weight of him on her felt like sex all by itself....

Late that afternoon, Alma soaked in Charlie's tub, looking at a picture book from The Englehook Historical Society. Charlie's house was included in one shot of the waterfront but the building Alma lived in had its own page. It was older than she or her landlord had thought—pre-Civil War—and had belonged to a family in the shipping industry. A summer place. Before that, the book said, the property had been home to a blacksmith's shop. Low, late afternoon sun poured into the bathroom windows as she towel dried her hair. It would frizz into a wild nimbus without her usual gel, but she hadn't thought that far ahead the night before.

I could really use some hair gel and some soap that doesn't light my poor, worn-out pussy on fire. Doc Bronner's Peppermint soap was one thing after a chaste night. But it was no friend to womankind after a night and afternoon of Charlie.

Alma had no desire to go back to her own place yet, though. She found her black and purple shirt in her bag, put it on over her jeans and went downstairs to see what Charlie had in his kitchen. She was looking forward to her turn cooking on his cool old stove—and impressing him with her skills.

Charlie bent over his stereo turntable and put on a record by a group called The Deseret String Band. "Utah group," he said. "Uncle Brad and Aunt Eleanor went out to Arches National Park just before they made that last trip to Tibet. This album was propped up next to the turntable when I moved in, still in its wrapper," Charlie said. "Songs of the Mormon pioneers. Thing's a hoot. I'm learning 'Railroading On The Great Divide.' Carter Family tune. You like?" He handed her the album cover.

"On Okedohkee Records," said Alma. "That's so funny." She listened to the pretty twinkling high notes of banjos and mandolins. "I can see why you like this stuff. It's super happy music."

She sat next to Charlie on the couch and let her eyes roam around the room to the hangings that must have come from India or Indonesia. A framed Grateful Dead poster from a concert they'd done at Cornell five years ago. And photos of Charlie with his hair short as a little boy. Charlie with his hair long in a graduation gown, flanked by two people who looked just like him. The kitchen, which faced west, was full of warm sunset light now, but it was already getting shadowy in the living room.

"Is the graduation picture you and your parents?"

"Me and my uncle and aunt. Dad wouldn't come up to Oswego to see me graduate. He was pissed off because I didn't want to be a doctor and I didn't want to be a stock broker. Mom was around but she kept having crying fits. So in case you think only *your* family is nuts…" He sighed. "Brad and Eleanor understood."

"You must really miss them."

Charlie nodded. "The whole issue with Dad was money, I think. He and I talk now, but it took a while. It's funny, Uncle Brad could have bought and sold Dad twenty times over. Retired at forty, he had made some terrific investments and cashed a bunch of them out. He had business cards made up that said Bradley Sassian, World Traveler, and proceeded to become one. He and Eleanor were even into the old-time fiddle stuff before I was." He cleared his throat. "So, what are we having for dinner, my dear private chef? You still up for cooking? You don't have to."

"You have decent canned tomatoes and pasta. And some really nice olives and anchovies. I could make pasta puttanesca," Alma said. "We wouldn't even have to go out and get stuff."

"I'd love that," said Charlie. A sound shook the house—like an air horn, but a million times louder.

"What the…" Alma stuck her fingers in her ears.

"Resolute Hose," shouted Charlie, in between the blasts of the fire horn. "Fire Department. Right … next door. You didn't … notice?"

"It was … dark. Yikes!"

"You get … used to it," said Charlie. "That's a 1-5-6."

There was a silence now.

"One five six?"

"Yeah. Fire code. One-fifty-six. They blow the horn first once, then five times, then—" It started up again. "*I'll tell you in a minute!*"

They waited until the fire horn stopped for good. "It's how the volunteers know where the fire is," Charlie said, and then there was more noise as two big, old-fashioned fire trucks with gold trim and round fenders pulled out of the firehouse next door and sped by in front of his house, sirens blaring.

"Wow! I never really noticed. I mean, I've heard the horn from a distance. I didn't know there was a code."

"I think it's pretty common up around here," said Charlie. "We had 'em downstate, too, but lots of towns stopped using them."

Alma nodded. Had there been a fire horn like that in Briarcliff? She remembered something left over from the Civil Defense paranoia of the 60s... "So how do you know the code?"

Charlie got up and opened the door above the basement stairs. He took a yellowed piece of paper off a hook on the back of it. "I thought *everyone* had one of these things," he said, running his finger down the page. "One-fifty-six. Maple Terrace and St. Marks. Isn't your place on St. Marks?"

"Yikes! That's like either the corner across the street from me or *my house!*"

"*No!*"

"Shit, shit, shit! I gotta..."

"Look, it's the night before Halloween. Gate night. Kids do stuff, you know? Probably just a pile of leaves in somebody's backyard."

"Charlie, I have to go see. I do. I'm sorry, but..."

"I totally get it. Let me drive, then." He got her grandfather's coat from his coat closet, and held it out for her to slide into. For himself, he grabbed a flannel-lined jean jacket, stuffing his long hair under it as they ran for the car.

Chapter Twenty

Alma and Charlie began to smell the smoke when they weren't too far past Bright Day School. It was thick by the time they got to the fire trucks on St. Marks Street. Red and blue lights flashed in the darkness and murk. Hoses snaked across the broad lawn in front of Alma's apartment.

"Oh, Charlie! Oh, shit!" Alma felt dizzy. Flames shot through her roof, and as she clicked open her seatbelt, a cedar tree near her kitchen window caught fire, too.

A few dozen neighbors stood silently in the road, arms folded, watching. Alma and Charlie stood in the yard. Charlie put an arm around Alma, and pulled her close to his side.

The house's second story was burning so brightly that it was hard to look at. But the first floor of the house seemed almost untouched. Alma searched her memory. She hadn't lit any candles the night before. Her stove hadn't been on, either. Of course not. She'd showered and left for Charlie's—after that awful scene with Bart. There had been ice in her apartment, not fire.

"Everybody please stay clear!" yelled a man with a helmet and fire-fighting gear on while a team of fire fighters trained a stream of water on the tree and put it out.

"Alma! Alma! Thank God!" shouted Alma's landlord. He'd been standing behind a fire truck with his mother. "Thank *God*. I tell 'em firemen I saw you go out last night. Thank God."

Peter's mother burst into sobs and pulled both Alma and Charlie into a hug. "Good girl!" she said, "Good girl!" Mrs. Koslov clung tightly to them.

The smoke was making it hard to breathe.

"Alma, I'm going go to talk to my pal, Frank Wanamaker, for a minute. He just showed up. Fire inspector," said Charlie, extricating himself. "I want to let him know you're okay. Be back in a second."

"Peter, Mrs. Koslov, I'm so sorry! I swear, I didn't leave anything turned on," said Alma.

"Not your fault, Alma! Not your fault!" said Peter. He took his mother's arm. The two of them watched the flames for a few more minutes, and then Peter led her away. His mother leaned heavily on him as she walked.

Charlie ran across the yard and put his arm back around Alma's shoulders.

Peter was talking to someone from the fire department about the electrician, how he'd just replaced the circuit breaker. "Good old house," said Peter, "Build 'em up strong!"

"Get *back!*" yelled another firefighter. The windows of Alma's apartment were burning even more brightly. It looked like the first floor might be catching, too. There was more smoke.

"Back!" the fireman yelled again. Charlie pulled Alma across the yard, and away from the house.

"Alma," he said. "Come stay with me. At my house. Please. As long as you want." He wrapped his arms around her, and Alma felt numb. The first place she'd ever lived in alone was vanishing before her eyes. Her poetry books from college. Her cookbooks. Her clothes and her knives. Everything she owned, except for a handful of clothing and her car. Yellow-white flames swam in her tears.

"Oh, shit, Charlie," she said. "Shit." She buried her head in his chest and closed her eyes. She could hear the fire roar, and the water from the hoses hissing as it hit the flames. The firefighters shouted, and somewhere behind her, Peter talked to his mother in a language Alma couldn't understand.

"It'll work out, Alma. You'll be okay." Charlie stroked her hair, and his gentleness finally undid her.

"I have to call work," Alma said, "and I have to … I have to…" She lost the rest of the sentence in sobs.

"I'll help you," he said. "I'll help you with everything. I will." Charlie's words were comforting, but she was still shaking. She closed her eyes. He held her, and stroked her hair … and then he stopped.

"Shit. Alma," he whispered. "Over there! Do you see? What the … *fuck*?"

Still wrapped in Charlie's arms, Alma turned around. Walking out of the house's open front door was the bright, translucent figure of a man in knee britches and a long dark jacket with many buttons. Bart had strapped his sword to his side, and he was making his way purposefully toward her and Charlie. His face was either sad—or filled with rage.

He strode by firefighters, cops, neighbors, and even a reporter from the local paper. No one seemed to see him. The reporter wore jeans and an orange corduroy jacket. She carried a camera and didn't even look up as Bart marched by inches in front of her.

But Charlie's eyes were huge, and they glittered in the blaze. "*Alma,*" he whispered again.

"Shh," said Alma. She stepped out of Charlie's arms. "Don't let on. I see him. I know."

"You *know?*" asked Charlie.

"Yeah."

Bart stopped in front of Charlie and gave him an odd half-bow. He rested a hand on his sword. "So. Shall I … *release* her to you, then, sir?" he asked.

"*What?*" said Charlie in a hoarse whisper.

Something crackled and thumped inside the house, but the flames seemed a little less intense, now. The reporter was talking to Alma's landlord. There were police cars, and an ambulance with Mrs. Koslov sitting inside it. In the flicker of the subsiding blaze, Peter waved off the reporter from the ambulance's door. The firefighters kept up their streams of water as the flames smoked more heavily—and then began to die. A few of the neighbors walked back toward their houses up the street.

"Let us be gentlemen about this matter. I release her," said Bart to Charlie. "To you, sir."

Release me? Alma was furious. "Bart, I do not *belong* to you," she hissed. "You can't release me. You have no right."

Bart bowed to Alma, too. "But I belong to *you*, Alma. I am your dead," he breathed. "*Your* dead! Don't you remember? I belong to you ... and therefore, you to me."

"I do not!" said Alma. "We don't belong to each other! We don't! You just ... *showed up* in my apartment and you..." She stepped farther away from Charlie. "You know what you did. Leave me alone!"

Charlie watched wordlessly.

Bart held his arms out to Alma, but the last thing she wanted was his embrace. "No! I mean it! Leave me *alone*," she said, but he grabbed both her hands instead. His touch was so cold that her knuckles ached right away.

"I *was* yours! I was! What we had *was real*. Admit that much!" Bart squeezed her fingers, and an icy buzz went up her arms and into her chest. She tried to pull away from him and couldn't. She remembered once when she was a little girl, plugging in a broken lamp she had found in her parents' basement. She'd had trouble letting go of it, her arm thrumming with electric shock when she finally did. Alma felt like that now, like she was being pulled into Bart ... like she could disappear. Like it would be a good thing for her to disappear. It would be so easy...

"No," she tried to say again, but nothing came out. Her mouth opened, but to her horror, she could barely catch a breath. She coughed.

"Admit it!" said Bart. "Admit it and release me!" Then he smiled, and his smile was proud and terrible. "Oh! Does this mean you will come along ... to where I must go?"

Alma managed to get some air in through her nose—but only a little. '*Where I must go,*' she thought. *He's going to dissipate. He wants me to...*

"Leave her *alone!*" Charlie's fist swung through the air. When it made contact with the side of Bart's face, there was no sound—and no effect. Bart still grasped Alma's hands fiercely.

Charlie shook out his fingers and glared.

"A kiss then, my sweet Alma," Bart said. "Come! Travel with me!"

She mustered the strength to shake her head no, struggling for another breath. Bart still gripped her fingers so tightly they were numb. He yanked her toward him. But Charlie had grabbed her shoulders, trying to pull her back and away. Charlie's hands were warm, and she was so cold. It would be so wonderful to be warm again! Though wouldn't it be much easier to just ... give in? Alma was much too tired to know what she wanted. Was the smoke getting heavier or was her vision beginning to fade?

Across the yard, the police cars pulled off.

Alma felt herself sway.

Bart still grasped her hands. "Alma!" he cried.

Alma shivered, gasped, and finally found her voice. "No, Bart," she said. "You have to go by yourself."

"But you are mine, Alma! I will *not!*" Bart shouted and this time his voice echoed weirdly, as if he were standing in an empty room.

Alma coughed again. "Go. Release *yourself!*" she said again. "I can't help you."

"No! No! *No!* Coward!" Bart suddenly let go of Alma's hands. His hands flew to the middle of his chest, and he groaned. She stumbled backward and Charlie caught her, wrapping his arms around her.

A trickle of bright red blood oozed between Bart's fingers. One hand still clutching his chest, he pulled his sword from his side and stabbed the empty air in front of him. The sword was bloody as he pulled it back. He collapsed onto the ground. All around him, firefighters and neighbors fought the fire and watched the fire and did not see.

Charlie held Alma as she bent over, coughing and trying to clear her throat. Her fingers prickled as the circulation worked its way back into them.

The Englehook Fire Department continued its work. The ambulance pulled off with Alma's landlord and his mother, red and blue lights flashing, but no siren.

A wind came off the river carrying a few brown maple leaves with it. It stirred up the few remaining embers in the house. A bright green light flared beside the place Bart had fallen, and then came Geoff's voice. "Such folly! Such *folly!*" The green light exploded into tiny sparks, and vanished. As he lay on the ground, Bart fumbled for his sword again, and then he was still. His glowing form became more and more blurred until there was nothing left of him but a pool of dull yellowish light. Then the light vanished, too.

"Still a little something going on up on that second floor, d'ya think maybe?" said one of the firefighters and kept his hose pointed up toward the place Alma had once lived.

Chapter Twenty-One

Alma sat up in Charlie's bed under the duvet and two quilts, finishing a mug of hot tea, lemon, and honey—with a healthy shot of bourbon in it. Her hands had almost stopped aching. She was back in her nightgown—Charlie's old tie-dye T. Charlie sat on the bed beside her, still in his Oswego sweatshirt. She remembered only a few scraps of the ride back from the fire.

"I didn't pass out?"

"No, but you weren't saying much," said Charlie. "You were mostly crying. At first I thought you were mad at me."

"Why would I be mad at *you?*"

"I don't know. Paranoid, I guess. You kept saying, 'I'm sorry,' so I decided you weren't. Mad at me, that is. But you were really unsteady on your pins. Which isn't so surprising considering…"

"My apartment and…"

"That ghost guy. Bart, I mean," said Charlie. "Wow. Never thought I'd actually see a…"

"Ghost guy? Yeah. Especially one I'd…"

"Dated?" said Charlie. "He seemed so … *possessive*. It's not like I'm jealous or anything."

Alma managed to giggle. Dated was such a tame word for what had happened. And possessive? As if Bart were any other man who'd gotten a bit too involved with her … except that's kind of what he was. Why was it suddenly funny?

Charlie smiled back at her. "It's really good to hear you laugh," he said. "I mean, that doesn't sound like *hysterical* laughter or anything. Which you would be perfectly entitled to. Yikes. Yikes to the tenth power."

"The ghost guy I … *dated!*" said Alma. She put

down her mug and guffawed.

"Look, I get it. I've had some pretty weird relationships myself," said Charlie. "And we both just watched him *die* or something. Can ghosts die? What the hell just happened? I tend to be pretty logical—sanitation and science and public health—like that, but I do try to stay open to the whole realm of…"

Alma snorted and laughed even harder. *I am laughing about something absolutely terrible,* she thought—but that only made it funnier. "Charlie," she said, but then she had to stop herself. Because she'd almost said, Charlie, I love you.

And I can't possibly be in love with someone after only… It has been three whole nights, now, she thought. *Well, two in the same bed.*

"He didn't exactly die. I think we saw him *dissipate*," Alma said, and speaking those words sobered her. *Thank God! Maybe I'm not a total monster.* "Ghosts call it that—dissipating. Bart told me that they sort of run out of energy after a while. I didn't think it was going to be so awful. He wanted to be gone, I think."

Charlie sipped his tea and whiskey before touching the back of his hand to her forehead. "Dissipate," he said and shook his head. "And he really wanted to take you along with him. You feel kind of normal, now. I guess. Hard to tell. I should have taken your temperature when we came in, before we had hot drinks. I wasn't thinking. You felt so cold! I actually thought emergency room for a couple of minutes, but you seemed to get a lot better once we got inside and I got some blankets on you. I figured the freak-out factor was lots of it…"

"Well, *yeah.*"

"So, that was Bartholomew what's-his-name, right?" Charlie said. "The one you always hear about from the old-timers in town? With the duel and everything? I figured because of the sword and the knee knickers and stuff."

"Yup." Alma shook her head. "And that green fireworks-looking thing, I think, was his dueling partner, Geoff. I think he must have dissipated, too. They were actually friends. As ghosts, that is. Maybe not so much in life. I … um … *told* you my house was haunted, Charlie."

Charlie made a raspberry noise that turned into laughter. "Ya think? Do we need another *soothing* cup of tea? I think maybe I could use one."

"Shit! I was going to cook you dinner tonight, Charlie! And double shit—I was supposed to call my mom today because my ex-husband is still dead. Oh, my God, I can't believe I said that. Except it's true. Plus—oh yeah, my apartment just burned down. And…" Alma snorted. "Oh, *fuck.* Why do I need to laugh again?"

"Because you're as warped as me, especially after you've had a good belt of whiskey?" said Charlie. "Alma. You are so incredibly, amazingly … don't get me started." He flopped over onto his side, put his arms around her and kissed her. His mouth tasted of hot tea and whiskey, and the feel of it lit her up inside. "Lovely woman, we haven't eaten since the doughnuts this morning. And you are *not* cooking dinner. I have macaroni and cheese in the freezer. My mom made it. I'm going to throw it in the micro-slave." Charlie grabbed their empty mugs and headed for the stairs.

A number of electronic peeps later, he walked carefully back into the bedroom holding a steaming mug in each hand. Alma accepted hers, sipped, and sipped again. Charlie's bed was getting cozier by the minute.

"You sure didn't hold back on the whiskey this time, did you?" Her lips buzzed with it, and she felt the heat in her stomach, too. It made her cheery, which was a little weird, but not unwelcome.

"Guess not," said Charlie. He pulled his sweatshirt over his head, revealing another tie-dye T underneath it.

Alma smiled. *Does he own a factory somewhere that pumps those things out? He is the king of tie-dye. And he even has a lava lamp over on his dresser! I didn't see that before. Too funny!*

She had a little more from her mug and looked up at the tall, long-haired man standing beside her. "Will you turn on your *lava lamp* for me, Charlie?"

"Turn on the *lava lamp?* Do you know what *that* means?" said Charlie. He found the lamp's on-switch and set his mug down next to it. He crouched on the foot of the bed, making growling noises. Long red hair spilled into his face as he freed it.

Alma growled back—and pulled his T-shirt off. Then she untied the string at the top of his sweat pants.

"Whoops!" said Charlie as his pants slipped down and she yanked off his shorts. After kicking his clothes asides, he sat beside her. "Goodness me. Never have I been so…"

Alma crawled into his lap, swamped in the oversized t-shirt he'd lent her. She wrapped her legs around him—and squeezed. "Perhaps I seem a bit … forward?" she said. "I wouldn't want to *offend!*"

His cock, standing at attention, did not seem a bit offended.

Charlie raised his eyebrows. "I am shocked and dismayed by your boldness." He removed her giant t-shirt and took her right breast into his mouth.

"*Oh.*" The heat of his tongue on her nipple sent a lightning bolt through her. Alma closed her eyes and savored it. Then, she stroked his cock and rubbed her finger in the wet that immediately formed at its tip. She was wet already, too.

Charlie moaned. He played with her other breast before helping Alma unroll a condom onto him. Sucking on his forefinger for a moment, he slid it into her, stroking her clit with his thumb.

"Oh, yes. Charlie, let me … here." She pushed Charlie backward on the bed until he was lying on his back, took his hand away, and eased his cock into herself. Straddling him and rocking, Alma felt even fuller than she'd been the night before. It almost hurt. But she was greedy for his thickness. She loved being in control of the heat between her legs. She set up a slow, steady rhythm, and bore down on him … carefully. There really was plenty of Charlie! He put his hands on her ass to steady her. She slowed down even more. And more.

"Oh, woman," said Charlie. "Oh."

The microwave pinged downstairs, and it didn't matter. They were moving so slowly they were almost still, and it hurt and it didn't. Alma squeezed Charlie's cock inside her until her orgasm began to flash. She tried to deny the sensation, but it flashed again, more deeply. Euphoria rolled over her until she couldn't control anything anymore.

"Yeah!" said Charlie. "Oh, yeah. I feel you coming!" His fingers dug into her and then he dissolved, too.

Alma teetered on tired arms above him, drooping her head.

"You are incredible," Charlie said. "Um, allow me to assist." He lifted her off him. "I just need to remove this thing … *there*."

When he came back from the bathroom, Charlie pulled the duvet back over them. "You seem *nice* and warm, now," he said, massaging her shoulders. "Sweet,

sweet woman. Since I'm *not* a chef who never eats, I am going *re*-nuke that mac and cheese. You want? I'll dump it on plates and bring it up with me."

"Re-nuked mac and cheese dumped on plates. Sounds perfect," said Alma.

Chapter Twenty-Two

Incredibly, Alma's apartment building was sound enough for the fire inspector to get into the next day. Charlie held Alma's arm as she picked her way up the stairs to what was left of her door. It wasn't hatchet-smashed, the fire had been so quick and hot that no one had been able to get to it. The first floor of the house, although uninhabitable, looked strangely undamaged, except for puddles of water everywhere. There were a few charred places, but mostly the walls were marked with smoke, and reeked of it, wet wood, and soggy cloth.

Frank Wanamaker, a tall man with a shock of prematurely silver hair and a brown leather jacket, was taking pictures of the damage in the Alma's old living room. The floor he stood on was still mostly solid. The windows were empty of glass, though, and the walls—where they still existed—almost completely blackened. Alma's furniture was barely recognizable. The ceiling was open to the sky in four or five places. Beyond the seared trees that stood near the house, the Hudson River was grey in cloudy mid-afternoon light.

"Mr. Frank-o!" called Charlie. "This is Alma Kobel. Alma, this is my excellent buddy, Frank. Plays wicked banjo and figures out the fires."

Frank reached out a hand for Alma to shake. "Didn't I see you at The Cracked Bell Thursday?"

Alma nodded, feeling numb. She wrapped her grandfather's black cashmere coat more closely around her as a cold breeze whipped through the empty windows. *That was my grandma's couch*, she thought, and kicked at the sodden remnant of a rug she'd really loved. *I could cry, and it wouldn't do me a damn bit of good.* Her nose stung with the stink of the fire. She blinked back her tears.

She felt Frank's eyes still on her. "Hey. It's *stuff*," he said. "That's all it is. I say that to people all the time and they never get it, but it's just stuff. I'm sorry it was your stuff this time. Pleased to meet you, and sorry it's under these circumstances. Important thing is you're okay. I just have to ask you a couple of things. Your landlord is taking full responsibility. He said you were a model tenant, and he knew the wiring was bad. Said he'd tried to fix it … but guess what? Guy owns half the cheap rentals in Englehook. He should know better."

"He was an okay landlord. He had an electrician in," said Alma. "New circuit breaker…" She tried not to think about what blew the lights in the house out when nothing much was drawing power—Bart.

I bet he made this happen.

"Yeah, yeah, yeah," said Frank. "Look at those walls. It's like an H-bomb went off inside them. Thank God you weren't home. This thing happened really fast and it was super-hot. The speed is the thing I don't quite get—but there is no trace of an accelerant. Peter Koslov wouldn't do that, anyway. He's a cheapskate, but no criminal. I did find plenty of highly messed-up wiring. Actually old knob and tube coming up from the basement and I think it was live! Stove was turned off, and what's left of the microwave looks like it was even unplugged, so nothing from the kitchen."

"Yeah," said Alma. "I used to pop fuses sometimes when I nuked stuff. After a while I got so nervous about the electric stuff in the house I disconnected it and just left it that way."

"I found something that could have been candles in the bedroom, but the pattern doesn't look like it started there."

"I didn't light candles last night," said Alma. "I came home from work, took a shower, and went out. I used my hair dryer, but I turned it off and unplugged it. Hung it on the back of the bathroom door."

Frank nodded, and wrote down a few words in a spiral notebook. "Yeah, I found something that looked like a hair dryer with a cord wrapped around it. Quasi-melted. Jesus."

"So, you think wiring?" That was Charlie.

"D'uh," said Frank. "Kind of a miracle with a fire this hot the whole building didn't go up. I have no idea how the wires got that hot. But the boys got on it right away. You probably saw the trucks take off from your place, Charlie, right? And you happen to be ... friends with Ms. Kobel?"

Charlie put an arm around Alma's shoulder. "Yes! She's my ... um ..."

Alma looked around the ruins of her apartment—walls gutted by the fire, odd shafts of light coming in through the holes in the roof—and suddenly felt the same crazy desire to laugh as she'd had at Charlie's house the night before. Better than crying, anyway. She took a deep breath. "He isss..." she said in the best fake-German accent she could manage, "...my *boyfriend*!"

"I am?" said Charlie, beaming.

"Frau Blücher!" said Frank. He made a noise like a horse whinnying. "*Young Frankenstein!* Great flick!"

"Yeah," said Alma, "and I don't even like flicks." She leaned against Charlie.

"That's Frahn-ken-*steen*!" Charlie said. "Alma's staying at my place, if you need to be in touch."

Frank tipped an imaginary hat to Charlie. "So, like I said, this one's pretty obvious," he said. "One freaky thing, though. You two gotta see this." He walked cautiously across the sooty floor, pointing at a shadow on a scrap of living room wall that still existed. Except it wasn't really a shadow—more of a place that seemed blacker than everything else, as if it had burned a bit more completely. "This freaked me right out when I caught it in the corner of my eye. You have to kind of squint a little ... stand over *here*."

"Oh, wow," said Charlie. "Yeah."

Alma put a hand over her mouth. She didn't have to squint at all. It was—almost—the figure of a person, about her height. Except it had no legs. Or head. She could make out the outline of a long jacket, two arms ... and was that a sword? She thought again of the circuit breaker, and the flashing lights, and the blackouts. *Bart. Bart did this. He totally did.*

"Spooky, huh?" said Frank. "It's like a torso. But there's absolutely no trace of any human being having been up here during the fire. You see weird stuff sometimes in my gig. Happy Halloween, kids!"

Alma felt Charlie take her hand and squeeze it.

"See you at The Cracked Bell Thursday, Frank," he was saying.

"Maybe I'll see you there, too," said Frank to Alma, "Ms..."

"Oh, for Heaven's sake, it's Alma," she said. She took one more look at the figure on the wall.

"And I can raise you at Charlie's? I'm almost positive I won't need to but..."

"Yeah, you can get me there," she said. "Otherwise, I'm chef at Bright Day. Just call the main switchboard, they'll put you through. I'm off tomorrow and Tuesday, though. Taking some personal time."

Frank nodded. "Sounds like a good idea. I'm really sorry about your apartment, Alma. Any friend of Charlie's is a friend of mine. I'll take a couple of more snaps and be on my way."

The clouds were breaking up a bit as Charlie turned the key in his ignition. He handed Alma a cassette.

"Want to hear some Jorma?" he said. "You know who he is, right? Oh, crap. That wasn't insulting, was it?"

Alma had been settling into a seriously funky mood, but she laughed. "It is Jorma KauKOnen or Jorma KAUkonen? Guy in Hot Tuna, right? I saw them once, in college. You have their poster in the room I stayed in the first night. The first night—wow. It's really only Sunday." She slid the cassette into the player, and a song called *Genesis* came out of the speakers. "Oh, that one is pretty."

"I always liked it, too," said Charlie. He pulled out of Alma's driveway onto St. Marks Street. "I'm figuring out a mando part for it. It's KAUkonen, by the way. Holy crap, Alma, that thing on the wall in your place—"

"Totally and completely creeps me out," said Alma. "Are you thinking what I am about the fire?"

"What are you thinking?"

"Oh, shit, Charlie, *Bart*."

"Absolutely."

"He started the fire. I know it." Alma sighed. "I just don't know what I was thinking. Doing what I did with Bart, I mean. God, Charlie. You have to understand—the whole thing was more or less a one-nighter."

Charlie didn't seem shocked. "He wanted more nights. I get that."

"When he got, um, amorous, the lights in the whole house would go out sometimes. Or they'd flash. That's why my landlord put in the new circuit breaker."

"Damn," said Charlie. "Okay, now I really want to punch that damn ghost again. Except punching him doesn't work, and he's all dissipated away anyhow, right? That sure looked like an exit last night."

"I think it *had* to have been." said Alma. "I thought I'd ended things with him, Charlie. I really did! But then he showed up in my apartment right before I came to your place Friday. He wanted me to help him get wherever he was headed by … um, jumping in the sack with him and burning up all of his energy. And he did *not* want to take no for an answer. Bet he lost it when I didn't come home the next day, and fried the apartment."

"He sure saved enough juice to come mess with you on his way to oblivion. And then he tried bringing you along for the ride. What a total and complete bastard." Charlie reached across the car and took her hand. "Know what? You've had some *terrible* luck with men, Alma."

Alma sputtered and then she burst into laughter. "Yeah," she said. "But I think my luck is changing—like, a lot. Hey, there's no way the ghost stuff is going to screw up your friend Frank or anything, right?"

Charlie frowned. "I don't think so. The way I figure, it's all electricity, right? That's what the nervous system runs on. Maybe it's what ghosts run on, too. Frank is saying the wiring caused the fire. Wiring equals electricity. Look, *I* saw Bart, too. But no way in hell am I going to tell Frank that I—"

"That's it! You can't without sounding totally nuts. And neither one of us would be *nuts* or anything, right? By the way, I need to stick my head into work," she said. "I promised Mary on the phone this morning. There's also a Bright Day kid I need to help with his Halloween costume. We should go back to your place and pick up my car so you don't get hung up there."

"I really don't mind," said Charlie. He signaled for a right turn.

"Really?"

"Really."

"Wow," said Alma. "I didn't expect you to… Wow, Charlie. I know these last few days have been a total shit storm," said Alma. "But major parts of it are actually fabulous."

Charlie grinned. "What's happening with us, Alma?" He took a quick left onto Marina Road and stopped under a still-schoolbus-yellow maple. After he undid his seat belt, he reached over for Alma's and swept her up into a long, gentle kiss. "What is *happening?*" he said again.

"I don't know," she said. She hooked his hair behind his ears, stroked his cheek, and kissed him back. The sun came out the rest of the way, then, and it was in her eyes when she opened them again. Squinting, she pulled down the visor and found herself smiling so hard her face hurt again.

"Alma, do you know what I think?" Charlie was blushing. "It's been like no time, but oh, man…" He shook his head. "Oh, *man!*"

"Yeah, same here," said Alma. "Me, too."

The river twinkled in the sun at the end of the block, and they watched it and listened to the music on the car stereo.

"So. Um. Did you decide about the funeral tomorrow?" said Charlie.

Alma sighed. "I really don't want to go, but I should. I didn't go to the wake. As you may have observed, I was somewhat… *occupied* yesterday. Stefan's friends all blamed me for the divorce. The wake would have been awful. But what kind of monster doesn't go to the funeral of a man she was married to?"

"You're not a monster." Charlie shook his head. "Alma, your *apartment* just burned up. Cut yourself some slack. Would anyone get any good out of it if you went?"

"That's the thing. My mom..." Alma sighed. "She adored Stefan. But..."

"She's *your* mom!" Charlie said. "She loves you. She should be thinking of you first!"

"She should," said Alma. And then Alma understood something she hadn't put into words before. "Charlie," she said. "I was barely out of college when Stefan and I got married. On our wedding night, after he fell asleep? I stayed up until about 5 AM reading Emily Dickinson. I knew I'd made this huge, colossal mistake. I think I went through with marrying him because I didn't want to disappoint Mom." Alma looked up at the brilliant tree they were parked under, and the yellow leaves blurred in her tears. "Oh, *shit*, Charlie," she said. "That was so dumb!"

And then she cried. Hard.

Charlie held her until a cloud blew over the sun and the afternoon dimmed again.

"I really *hate* crying," said Alma, finally, and stopped.

"It's supposed to be good for you. But yeah." Charlie opened his glove box and she shook her head as he found two three-packs of Kleenex neatly stacked on top of a perfectly folded map. Next to a food thermometer in a spotless plastic carrying case. "I know. I know," he said, as he dried Alma's cheeks. "Always super-duper prepared. I'm just..."

"You're just amazing." Alma took a Kleenex from Charlie and wiped her nose.

"I don't know whether it's Health Department or Boy Scouts or..."

Alma smiled. "I think you maybe just like shopping in the drug store or something. Actually, we should go there. I need hair gel. And soap that doesn't irritate the hell out of my … um… Yikes." She shook her head again, this time so hard the hair flew into her eyes. "I don't know what's going on, Charlie. I feel terrible and then I feel great and then…"

"Alma?" he said. "I love you. I'm very sure of it."

Alma gasped. But she found herself smiling so hard her face hurt again. "I love you, too," she said. "I'm … very sure of it, too. God, Charlie! I didn't even know what it felt like before!"

"Me, either."

They kissed again until Alma thought her heart would burst.

Chapter Twenty-Three

The wind blew Alma's coat open as she took Charlie's hand and led him into the Bright Day main building.

"Let me go in first," she said to him. "I told Mary about us on the phone this morning, but I'm not sure what she shared with Jo Beth. Don't want to scare anybody."

"Scare? Oh, right," said Charlie. "My job. Duh."

"Yeah," Alma said.

Mary in her kitchen whites stood at the deep fat fryer, a green paisley scarf over her head. She carefully lowered two baskets of chicken drumsticks into the oil. Alma waited to say, "Trick or treat," until the hissing and bubbling quieted down, but Mary still jumped. Her friend pursed her lips and nodded at her.

"Well, would you look at that?" Mary said. "How are you doing, lady?"

"I guess I could be a lot worse."

Mary wiped her hands on a towel she'd tossed over one shoulder and hugged her. "I really *am* sorry about Stefan, babe. I know the guy couldn't keep it in his damn pants, but still. Human being and stuff."

Alma's eyes burned a bit. *Stupid tears.* She blinked them back.

"And your *place* at the same time! I still can't get over that. Holy freakout, Batman. Oh, *Alma!*" She hugged her harder.

"Yeah," said Alma, swallowing down the tightness in her throat. "Really. I'll be okay. Thanks for filling in for me tomorrow and Tuesday. Scrambled eggs and Kaiser rolls for breakfast tomorrow and how about tuna melts for lunch? Put out some potato chips, make the kids happy. There should be greens downstairs for salad. I think I ordered bread already, but I'll call and check. I've been a bit distracted."

Mary stepped away from Alma and gave the handles of the fryer baskets a shake. She peered into the bubbling oil. "A bit distracted. Yeah, I guess. You are way too good at keeping it together, Alma," she said.

"No I'm not," Alma said. "And like I told you … it hasn't *all* been terrible with me."

"It smells like Heaven in here," said Charlie.

Mary wheeled around and put her hands and her hips. "Mr. Charlie Sassian, you *dog!*" She threw her head back and laughed.

Charlie looked flummoxed for a minute, then he laughed, too. He pecked Alma on the head.

"Awww," said Mary. "Now are you sure that's really … *sanitary*? Germs! Germs!"

Alma snorted.

"Hey. It's the weekend," said Charlie. "Those drumsticks done yet?"

"Incoming!" Jo Beth Gooden shoved open the door of the kitchen with a cardboard carton full of cabbages and red onions. "Oops! We've got company!" She dropped the carton on the counter, tightened the bandana over her unruly silver hair, and hurried to the sink to wash her hands.

"He's defanged, Jo," said Mary. "Harmless. Remember what I told you about Alma and—"

"*Harmless?*" said Charlie. "Not sure I like that."

"Oh, fabulous," Alma rolled her eyes, "I'm hot gossip." But she wasn't angry. She was actually rather proud.

There was the sound of a racing BMW from the dining room—or rather, Benny imitating one. Charlie looked puzzled again.

"That's Benny," said Alma. "I gotta go in there

and see him." She dropped her voice to a whisper. "He likes to pretend he's a car. He's in the vocational program."

"Thinks he's a BMW," whispered Mary, and cleared her throat. "If you want, I can make you up a little takeout," she said in her normal voice. "Just an intimate little nibble for you two honey bears—Oh look at you *blushing!*"

"Shut up," said Alma. "But I probably got way too much chicken, for real. I'll take a bit with me. Thanks. Place looked kind of empty on our way in. Lots of kids home for Halloween?"

"Yeah. Probably we're down at least thirty."

"Yikes! It would help if they *told* me things like that before I ordered," said Alma.

"I wouldn't sweat it," said Mary. Bright Day didn't mind spending money for food. Staff got take-out from time to time. And the school's owners were not above middle-of-the-night kitchen raids. They lived in town.

"So. I told you I'd come in, and here I am," said Alma. "You're set up for Monday. I'll get the ordering done from Charlie's place. What else can I do for you, lady?"

"Nothing. I just wanted to see you being okay. Your *house* burned down. I was worried. They know what caused the fire yet?" She pulled the fryer baskets out of the fat and shook them again. Then she looked hard into Alma's eyes.

Alma looked back at her just as hard. *I wonder if she thinks what I think.*

"Wiring," said Charlie, firmly. "We just came from there. You know Frank Wanamaker, the inspector? He's on it."

"Frank? Yeah, we've met," said Mary, dumping

the drumsticks onto a rack to drain. "Let's see. Let's do *breasts*, next, I guess. And then … *thighs!*" She raised her eyebrows at Alma and smiled.

"You are bad," said Alma. "C'mon, Charlie, there's someone I want you to meet." They walked into the dining room, where Benny had just about finished setting the tables. He was wearing his Money Helps t-shirt again, and as usual, his long blond hair was tied back in a pigtail.

"Alma!" Benny waved. "Mary told me your house went on fire! I saw the fire trucks. They drove right by here." For a moment, Alma wondered if Benny was going to imitate them, but he didn't. "I'm sorry that happened to you," he said instead.

"Thanks, Benny," said Alma. "This is my friend Charlie."

"Hi, Charlie," said Benny. He made a small engine rumble. Beemer, not emergency vehicle.

Alma ignored it. "When do you get to put on your costume and makeup?"

"In about five minutes," said Benny. "I'm setting up now so I can go back to my group. Can I have the chef hat?"

"I came in because I wanted to be the one who gave it to you." They walked back through the kitchen and into the stockroom, and Alma picked out one of her toques for Benny. "Here you go, Benny," she said. "Now you can be Monster Chef!"

"Thanks!" Benny ran out through the back of the kitchen.

Alma and Charlie walked behind him. Jo Beth was tossing pineapple coleslaw in a big, stainless steel bowl.

Mary slid two big paper bags over the counter toward Alma. "Here you go, you crazy kids," she said.

"Dinner for two. You'll have trick or treaters, right? I hear you have a whole house all to yourself, Charlie!"

Charlie smiled. "That I do."

"Thanks again, Mary," said Alma. "Yeah, Charlie. Do lots of kids show up at your house on Halloween?"

"Four or five big bags of candy worth," Charlie said. "If I don't want my pumpkin smashed, we'd better get back there. The little ones start coming around with their parents before it's even dark."

They got back in Charlie's car. "I am drooling," he said. "How much chicken did Mary give us?"

Alma opened one of the bags sitting on her lap. "Oh, God, it does small amazing," she said. "We've got plenty. Some of that slaw, too. And what's this? Oh, yeah. Jo Beth made bread pudding. We are set up."

"Excellent." Charlie grinned. "By the way, that Benny kid is kind of sweet. Does he really think he's a BMW?"

"I don't think so. He likes to pretend he does, though. We call him Benny the Beemer. We're not supposed to, but it makes him happy. His roommate, Roy, hit me over the head with a loaf of whole wheat bread because I made French toast instead of pancakes one morning. It was kind of hilarious. I love my job."

"I love my *life*," said Charlie. "Who doesn't like French toast?"

Alma laughed. "Roy. For real."

Chapter Twenty-Four

Alma's right hand had fallen asleep. She'd been on the telephone with her mother for almost half an hour. Philomena had gone from sobbing about the wake to dark hints about having foretold Stefan's death and back at least three times. Alma's news about her apartment had undone her, too—almost as much. Philomena said predicted that, too, of course.

"That man in my dream! He was going to carry you off! That had to be about the *fire!* Thank God, you had gone out. Now, you say you are staying with…"

Yuck. The worst thing was that her mother was sort of right. If the man in her dream had been Bart, well… She shuddered. Or, of course, her mother could also have made the whole thing up. Still…

"I'm staying with Charlie Sassian," Alma said. "He works for the local Department of Health. Yes. Yes. I know him through my job." Downstairs, she could hear him dumping Halloween candy into bowls. "Charlie has … a very nice house," she said. She hadn't even been able to get to the part about not planning to go to the funeral yet.

"Alma?" called Charlie from downstairs. "Want to help carve a pumpkin?"

"I'm still talking to my mom." Alma smiled. *Charlie actually buys a pumpkin for his front porch and carves it for trick or treaters,* she thought. *Instead of going out to a bar and hoping to leave with some girl in a sexy nurse costume.*

"Oh, I'm keeping you," said Philomena. "So, I'll see you tomorrow?"

Alma took a deep breath. "Mom, I don't think I can. I just lost my apartment. I have to buy some clothes to wear, for one thing. I haven't even had a chance to do that. And I'm kind of … *upset*, about things, you know? I know we were married, but Stefan's lawyer kept me poor for almost two years. And then you gave Stefan my address and he came up to my place out-of- control drunk and—"

"Oh, honey, I could loan you a simple black dress. Just put on any old thing and drive right down here now. You can stay over with us. It'll be fun! I don't know why you have to be staying with a *stranger* when you have *family!*" It was like Philomena had only heard what she wanted to hear.

Not so unusual. "Charlie's no stranger, Mom. I've been *seeing* him." *There. I told her*. Alma almost had to bite the inside of her lip to keep from laughing. "Seeing" was as much of an understatement as "dating" for what had actually been going on.

"*Oh.*" Her mother's voice was cold now. "I see. You have a new boyfriend and you're not coming to poor Stefan's *funeral!*"

That was enough. Alma's patience snapped. "Stefan came up here to harass me. I told you he was drunk on his ass. We're damn lucky he didn't kill someone driving home. I'm sorry he died, but he's not 'poor Stefan.' He cheated on me and laughed about it. You're *my* mother and you're going to have to understand that. Besides, I have a job to do up here. I took time from work to get my life back together after the fire, but I have orders to place and I—"

"Stefan died of a *broken heart!* Over you! He wanted you back, Alma! *Please* come tomorrow."

"Stefan died because he fell down the stairs drunk," said Alma. "And his friends can't stand me. There's no reason for me to be there, Mom."

"Maybe you wouldn't worry about your job— your *money*—so much if you knew he left you the

Randolph Dye Works Triptych!"

Alma winced as she remembered three huge paintings. Brick buildings with graffiti on them and all their windows smashed out. Trees with plastic bags caught in their bare branches. Rusted-out dumpsters. Now she'd have to ... *do* something about them. The triptych was art that Stefan had cared about and she'd be respectful. But ugh.

"That was *very* generous of him," said Alma. "But I do have to go now. Mom, this isn't about you. It's about me. I'm sorry Stefan died, but I'm not coming down. Tell Dad I'm his girl. I'll see you at Thanksgiving."

She hung up the phone.

Downstairs, Charlie had already gotten most of the seeds and goop out of a very large pumpkin that sat on his kitchen counter as the light in the windows was going blue.

"Wow. That sounded unpleasant," said Charlie. "Couldn't help but hear."

"It was more than unpleasant," Alma said. "I am absolutely, positively not going to that funeral. If I had ever thought about maybe driving down there, it's totally out of the question, now. Oh, smart of you to use that ice cream scoop to clean out the pumpkin. Hand it over. I need to blow off some steam." Charlie gave the scoop, and Alma went after the rest of the pumpkin guts, teeth clenched. "Brains!" she said. "Brains!"

"Happy or scary?"

Alma looked at Charlie blankly. She'd put down the scoop, and was pulling out the rest of the seeds and stringy glop with her fingers. "Oh, the pumpkin's face." She blew out a long, slow breath. "Happy, actually. I wasn't so sure for a minute." She kissed Charlie on the cheek, holding her pumpkin-slimed hands away from him.

He wrapped his arms around her and rocked her back and forth. "Me, too," he said. "Happy, I mean." Then, the doorbell rang. "And away we go." He grabbed a bowl of candy.

Three hours later, the grade school princesses, angels, ghosts, and robots with their smiling parents had morphed into embarrassed-looking high school kids with faint attempts at costumes and pillowcases full of candy bars. Alma and Charlie had both managed to put away a fair amount of Mary's excellent fried chicken in between trips to the door. She had just popped the bread pudding into the oven to warm up.

"Got some cream I could whip for the bread pudding?" she called in to him from the kitchen.

"Nope. But check the freezer. I think there's Häagen-Dazs vanilla back in the frozen wastes." Charlie's "frozen wastes" happened to be a bunch of neatly labeled containers of soups and a big package of venison. *Of course.* She was getting to the point where she wasn't surprised anymore at Charlie's tidiness or his well-supplied house. There was a set of hand-thrown pottery bowls on a shelf by the sink. Alma split the bread pudding between two of them and topped each with a scoop of ice cream.

"These bowls are pretty," Alma said, carrying them in.

"Aunt Eleanor made them. There's still a lot of her pottery in the house." He stuck a spoon in his bread pudding and put some in his mouth. "Oh, man. What did Jo Beth put in this? I could eat a whole tray."

"Grade B maple syrup, actually. You know, the Blanchards, the folks who own the school? They think it's healthier than white sugar. Stuff is pretty delicious. People pay extra for Grade A, but it's not as good."

The doorbell rang again. Alma opened it to a pair of high school kids in actual costumes, a boy and a girl, their faces painted like the rock band, KISS.

"Wow," said Charlie, dumping a handful of peanut butter cups into their bags. "I thought you guys broke up after your last album."

"Never!" said the boy.

"Yeah, we're still touring," said the girl. "Thanks!"

"Yeah, thanks," he said. They skipped off the porch together, laughing and holding hands.

"Aw," said Alma. "Young love. KISS, though? *Really?* I kind of thought they broke up, too."

Charlie put an arm around her. "If this is like most Halloweens, we've got maybe another twenty minutes. Or maybe not even. Things usually go dead around nine. Then, you get the big kids out trashing stuff, but not much of that happens down here. Sometimes they get my pumpkin, sometimes not. I think it's the fire department next door. They keep their lights on pretty late."

"That was fun. Kids don't trick or treat in apartment buildings much." Alma looked out at the sidewalk in front of Charlie's house and to the river and the lights on the other side. She could hear laughter in the distance, but the street was finally empty.

"Want to go upstairs?" asked Charlie. "I've got to hit the sack pretty early. I *don't* have a personal day tomorrow. I'm glad you're not going down to that funeral."

"Oh, God, me too," said Alma. "I'm going to sleep in a little and then I have to start replacing my clothes, I guess. It's really weird not owning anything. It's kind of not terrible, though. I get to start from scratch and just get the things I like. Luckily, the divorce stuff is done, so I can almost afford it."

"Come away from the doorway a minute."
Charlie pulled her into a long kiss and rubbed her back.
"Alma, don't be in a hurry about things. Stay here as
long as you want. Get on your feet. I meant what I said
last night. I like it when you're here."

"I like it when I'm here, too," said Alma. "Should
we blow out the pumpkin?"

"Yeah, I think it's time," said Charlie.

Chapter Twenty-Five

Alma and Charlie were asleep—hard asleep—by twenty after ten. But just after eleven something opened Alma's eyes. She'd been having nightmares. Bright Day food orders not coming in, the fryer at work catching on fire, and then a less dramatic but more horrifying one— she was still married to Stefan. The phone was ringing, and he was holding her down by the wrists to keep her from picking up the call, which she knew was for her. Then, he turned into Bart. She understood it was a dream just before she woke up from it, shaking.

She inhaled and exhaled slowly, letting the reality of where she was sink into her again. A dull blue glow barely illuminated Charlie's white curtains. The lava lamp was still on and burbling purple and green, Alma watched it for a few minutes, and it made her smile. Charlie lay next to her with a pillow stuffed under one arm and his hair everywhere.

She resisted the temptation to stroke his head. *He's got to get up early*. She curled up closer to him and enjoyed the fact that his room was becoming familiar to her. *It sounds like Charlie wants me to live with him.* Then she thought about how proud she'd been when she finally got her own place and felt weepy again. *But he loves me. And I love him. I guess this all works out somehow, eventually.*

She was about to close her eyes again when she saw the green light in the hall. And started a little.

Only Charlie's nightlight.

But then it moved, and the shadows changed in the bedroom.

Alma knew what it was right away—or more to the point, *who* it was. She slid out of bed, a nicely washed-out, extremely oversized Jefferson Airplane t-shirt flapping around her legs. And smelled pipe smoke.

"Hello?" she whispered.

Geoff sat on the top of the stairs, glumly smoking. The green glow around him seemed a little dimmer than usual, but it still made weird shapes in the stairwell and reflected in the hall window.

"I thought you'd dissipated," she said.

Geoff shook his head no.

"Um, I think you should smoke that thing outside. Let's talk on the porch and not wake Charlie."

"Charlie," Geoff said, rolling his eyes.

Alma frowned. "Shhh! He's got to get up early," she whispered, and looked nervously at the bedroom door. But Charlie didn't stir. The only other sound was the refrigerator humming in the kitchen. "C'mon," whispered Alma, and padded downstairs barefoot. After a moment, Geoff followed her. She silently turned the knob on the hall closet and got out her grandfather's black coat. They sat down in the two rocking chairs on the front porch, beside the extinguished jack o' lantern.

"Why are you here?"

"I'm not sure," said Geoff. "I thought I was on my way out with Bart. He certainly gave me another good run-through with the sword. I felt the cold for the first time since I was in life. But then I woke up in downtown Englehook a few hours ago with all those tiny imps swarming around, every last one of them groggified on sweets. If I hadn't been so weary I'd have terrified a few."

"Bart really *did* dissipate, didn't he?"

Geoff sighed. "That he did."

They sat together quietly for a few minutes. Geoff blew a few green luminous smoke rings.

"I'm sorry, Geoff. I didn't…"

"How could you have known? He could be very

charming, the scoundrel. What he did with you was wrong, and I beg your forgiveness for my part in it. Bart always was reckless around women."

And you weren't? It seemed unkind to remind him of that now. "Last night," she said. "Bart wouldn't let go of me. He wanted me to go along with him. Could he actually have…"

Geoff grimaced. "He certainly could have. Crying to me about his broken heart and then pulling you along with him into oblivion! Such a great, loveless fool! You were in danger, so I did what was needful. I sent my friend Bartholomew into a land even ghosts do not know. And thought I should surely follow him because of it. We were not play-acting this time."

"And you?" said Alma.

Geoff shrugged. "I may well be nearly spent."

It was very still, and Alma could hear the little waves on the river. She said nothing for a minute. Then, she got out of her rocker, and stood in front of Geoff. "Thank you," she said. "Really. Thank you so much." She waved away a smoke ring, bent down, and kissed him on the cheek. He felt oddly un-ghostly, neither warm nor cold, and a little whiskery. She smiled. "It's okay that you stole my flour and trashed the bread order. Thank you for my life."

The wind blew, and with it came the sound of a church tower in town, tolling midnight.

Geoff put his fingertips to his lips, and then patted Alma's cheek. He smiled, too. "And now you have that big red-headed oaf to keep you company. Which is meet and right, as they say. Farewell, then." The green glow around him grew fainter and fainter, until it flashed brightly—and then disappeared. There was an odd squelching noise, a thump—and then a wicked chuckle. Nothing was left of Geoff but his voice.

"Alas! Some vile ruffian has smashed your pumpkin, m'lady!" it said. He chuckled again, and was gone.

Alma wrapped her coat around herself. She sat and looked at the river for a few minutes, and then she heard footsteps inside. Charlie stuck his head out onto the porch.

He was big and red-headed, but he certainly didn't look like an "oaf" to Alma.

"*There* you are!" he said. "What are you doing *outside?* It's freezing!"

"Long story," said Alma. She felt a little tearful again. She got up and hugged him. "Let's go back to sleep. I love you, Charlie. I just wanted to say that again."

Charlie beamed. "I just wanted to *hear* you say that again. I love you, too." He started to pull her inside but stopped. "Oh, shit, Alma! Somebody smashed our pumpkin!"

Chapter Twenty-Six

It was odd but lovely being alone in Charlie's house that next day. Alma woke up when he left and kissed him goodbye. After that she went back to sleep hard until about ten, gathered up a load of her dirty clothes to wash, and found a stack of legal pads in the carefully refinished mahogany desk downstairs. Sitting up in bed with a cup of coffee in what had to be an Aunt Eleanor thrown mug, she set about trying to reconstruct the week's menu and figure out what needed to be ordered. It wasn't hard, really—a call to Pete at Hudson Market helped lots—and he was super sympathetic about her apartment. Another call to Mary at Bright Day and things were in good shape at work.

She found a pair of Charlie's sweat pants in his dresser, so big and long they came up underneath her breasts. She put them on underneath her "nightgown" and padded back downstairs.

Funny how fast fall turns into winter up here. The air outside was chilly and grey, but it was cozy at the kitchen table. She poured herself another cup of coffee, listening to the clothes dryer tumbling in the cellar. Soon her jeans would be dry, and she'd go out and buy some clothes.

That'll be fun. Alma vowed that the first thing she would replace would be what she'd just bought plenty of—underpants. From now on, cotton or bust! Sale or no sale at the outlet store, no more bits of silk, string, and stiff, scratchy frills! The black lace number she had on at the moment was riding up under the sweat pants, which would have been funny if it weren't mildly painful. Sexy undies plus new relationship equals ouch. On her way back upstairs for a shower, she stopped for a moment to take in the house's well-organized, comforting Charlieness. And smiled.

The phone rang then, and she sat on the bed to pick it up.

"Hey," said Charlie's voice. "I wanted to call the house and have you answer."

"Hey," she said. "You must have read my mind. I was thinking about you. So, um—how's work?"

"Just got back from really laying down the law at Sokolov's, actually, so it's been kind of intense. They have a really gross rodent problem. They're not out of business completely, but they've got some real work to do if they want to sell any more sausage."

"Oh dear. My poor old landlord. First the fire, and then this. He loved their kielbasa. He used to give it to me for presents."

"You *ate* that stuff?"

"Well, yeah. It was actually kind of good."

Charlie snorted. "The rat poop adds that certain je ne sais squat."

"Wow, Charlie! That was disgusting. I didn't think you had it in you. I am impressed."

"You wouldn't believe what else I have in me.' He dropped his voice to a growly whisper. "I'll be home by six."

Alma decided that minute she'd make her pasta al forno for dinner, which could sit in the oven a good long time if something else got heated up. She took her happiest shower in many months, glorying in the gentle glycerin soap she'd finally remembered to pick up, and the fact she had pretty much decided she would keep living with Charlie. *Outside of certain worn out areas, I feel kind of great. Maybe I should trust it.*

But then her mood darkened. It was almost noon. Stefan's funeral would be just starting, down in Westchester. Because her mother had planned everything with Stefan's brother, the service was going to be at Trinity Church in Ossining, where Alma had gone as a little girl. Trinity was Episcopal, and they used lots of incense. Alma pictured clouds of smoke in the air—and a coffin with Stefan inside it. Or would he have been cremated? "I don't even know," she said aloud, to the showerhead, and the loudness of her own voice in the bathroom startled her a little. *What kind of monster isn't even sad*, she thought. *What kind of monster actually feels ... relieved?*

She gelled and dried her hair, wrapped herself up in Charlie's bathrobe (*note to self: buy bathrobe*), and got her laundry out of the basement. Then, she opened the curtains in the bedroom for some natural light to put on her eyeliner. Alongside the Hudson, many of the trees were empty and the river reflected them. The water shimmered in the dull midday light. *The leaves are down along the river shore.* Then she said the words out loud, counting the rhythm of them on the fingers of one hand. Five strong beats—iambic pentameter. The first line of a poem. She ran downstairs for paper and wrote it down. *It's been almost ten years since I actually wrote a poem.* And then she cried.

By four o'clock, Alma was back at the house with a two bags of groceries, three pairs of jeans, a pair of leggings, five new shirts, and a really nice green and black checked turtleneck sweater that came down past her hips. She hadn't forgotten a flannel bathrobe or some unglamorous but comfortable cotton undies either. All the basics were covered. She'd worry about fancier stuff next paycheck.

She stood in the kitchen, slicing mushrooms for the baked pasta. She'd already CuisinArted the Parmesan cheese. Of *course* Charlie had a food processor—either barely used, or very carefully maintained. It was fun putting dinner together for just two people and almost no work, compared to her job. Once the al forno was ready for the oven and the romaine hearts salad was in the fridge, she sat back down with the poem.

Charlie burst into the house at twenty minutes after five, bearing long-stemmed red roses. "*Hello!*" he sang. "For you. I didn't cheap out this time." Alma accepted the flowers and felt her eyes fill up for the second time that day.

"Nobody gave me actual roses before," she said. "Long stems and everything. Seriously. I'm all..." She sniffled.

"*Nobody?*" said Charlie. "What's wrong with this world? And what do I smell? Have we moved to Milan? Venice?"

"Sort of a lasagna thing I used to make at Alberto's," Alma said. "I really like your stove, by the way."

"*Now* I know why I bought that thing. Let me get out of these work duds." He ran upstairs and came back a few minutes later with his hair loose, in a hand-knit Irish sweater and jeans.

"Cool sweater," said Alma, trimming the bottoms of the roses and fitting them into a tall glass vase she'd found under the sink. "You could wear *that* to work, you know."

"Thanks. The polo shirts are ugly on purpose, kind of. A uniform. I copied what the other guys wear to work." Charlie grinned. "I like that black and green thing on you. New?"

Alma nodded. Charlie's sweater felt soft and warm under her fingers when he hugged her, and she lost herself in kissing him.

"Oh, my. Oh, my! Let us proceed to the living room with a glass of wine. Would it upset you if I lit a fire?" he said. "I was afraid to yesterday because—well, you know."

"Sure," said Alma. "It's cold out. I'm okay with a fire as long as the flames stay where they belong."

Charlie arranged some logs in the fireplace. "Your house made the paper. Want to see?" He held out a copy of that week's *Englehook Informer.*

Alma's stomach tightened. The headline said *Gate Night Blaze* and there it was—her apartment with flames shooting through its roof. The picture made her sadder than she'd expected. She read the article beneath it.

"Hah," she said. "At least Peter and his mom had another place to stay. I guess she was more freaked out than sick. It says she was 'treated and released' at the hospital."

"They don't even mention *you* until like four paragraphs in," said Charlie. "I like how they said you'd be 'staying with a friend.' My brush with fame! The reporter must have gotten that piece from Frank. I don't see us in that picture. Do you? We'd have been right *there*—just beyond where it cuts off."

Charlie got up and poked at the fireplace, and the smallest of the logs began to smoke. "I couldn't stop thinking about all that crazy stuff with Bart today," he said. "Things were happening so fast this weekend I was just kind of surfing over them. Are you freaked out? I mean—that and your ex…"

"I'm kind of freaked out that I'm not *more* freaked out," said Alma. "Mostly I feel relieved. Sad about my place but…" She held the paper closer, but then she frowned. "Oh, shit. Look at *this*, Charlie," she said, pointing to what looked like a small balloon, or a tiny, glowing ball. A slightly larger one floated next to it, in the lower right corner. "Isn't this right in front of where we were?"

"I think. Looks almost like the camera had a light leak or something." Charlie went to his desk and opened a drawer. He found a magnifying glass, handed it to Alma, and sat back down beside her on the couch.

She squinted at the picture through the glass. Inside one of the balloons was something that looked like Bart's face, mouth open, either laughing … or screaming. In the other orb was a pair of hands, stretched outward. "Oh, shit," she said, and dropped the paper. "Shit, shit, shit. That's enough. That's quite enough." She handed Charlie back the magnifying glass.

"What?" he said. 'What was there?" He looked through the glass at the picture. "That kind of looks like *hands*, doesn't it? And the other…" Charlie shook his head. "Look, Alma. It's gotta be a glob of ink from printing. We could just be bringing the story we remember into this. Frank knows Patty D'Attore, who wrote that piece. We could get the original photo and look. We should—"

"Please," said Alma. "Let's *not*. I really hate thinking about it, and now I can't think about anything else. It could have been way worse. I was waiting for the right time to tell you about what got me out on the porch last night." She told him about Geoff.

"Holy crap," said Charlie. He shook his head. "No words," he said, and stared into the fire for a few minutes.

"I thanked him a whole lot."

"Wish it could have been *me*," said Charlie. "Doing the saving, I mean."

"You know what? It was. I saved myself, too. I think it was a group effort."

"So Geoff is really gone, this time? Dissipated, I mean?"

"He said he was 'nearly spent' and he said 'farewell.' He was the one who smashed the pumpkin, by the way. Because he's Geoff. Or was."

Charlie looked up at the ceiling. "Geoff, just in case you're still around—thank you!" Alma almost expected the lights to flicker. Or for something to spill, or break. But nothing did.

"Charlie?" she said. "I wrote this today. For you. I told you I was serious about poetry in college? I really thought that was what I was going to do with my life. Pretty naive, I guess, but my folks liked the idea, especially my mom. Follow your dreams and all that crap. Of course, I couldn't write anything the whole time I was married to Stefan. I thought I'd kind of lost it. It's been ten years." She gave him a piece of yellow legal paper.

"You wrote me a *poem?*"

"Yeah."

He handed it back to her. "Want to read it to me?"

Alma put her hands in front of her face. "I can't."

Charlie smiled, and turned a little red. "Oh, man. This looks like a sonnet, Alma. You wrote me a sonnet!"

"It's just a first draft. Like I said, it's been years. I'm really rusty." Alma blushed, too. And then she thought, *He knows what a sonnet is.*

For Charlie, the sheet read.

The leaves are down along the river shore
but yet the river, living, holds the light.
It glitters, breathing less and breathing more,
beneath the empty trees. And on toward night,

it gathers darkness like a gentle word
that comforts us to sleep. The tide flows by

and then reverses, sparkling and blurred:
a rippled moon, a starry rippled sky.

When I awake and you are sleeping still,
I watch the Hudson, grateful for what's new,
astonished there's a coming day that will
lend me the luck to write these words to you.

Astonished that I'm here—and also free
in loving you, to joy in what will be.

Charlie read the poem and looked back into
Alma's eyes. "I think... I don't even *know* what I think.
Wow, Alma. Thank you. This is pretty incredible.
Um..." He stared into the fire.

"Um, what?" said Alma.

"Does this mean that you're going really to live
here?"

"It seems crazy, but—um, are you asking me to?"

"Kind of sounds like it, doesn't it?" Charlie
pulled Alma into his lap and squeezed her close. "We
love each other," he said. "Who'da thunk!"

Chapter Twenty-Seven

The next Saturday morning, Charlie and Alma drove down to Stefan's loft to meet Alma's mother and Stefan's agent. "I can't believe I'm back in Kingston," said Alma as they got out of the car in front of the tall brick building where Stefan had lived. "I haven't been in this place since the night I found Stefan in the bathtub with that … child. She was one of his students, you know."

"Weren't you?"

"Nah. I didn't take his classes. Mary, who works with me in the kitchen? She had Stefan. That's how I met him. He lived here, and if you were cool you got invited to his parties. Or should I say, if you were female, you got invited to his parties. I used to think the main reason he got involved with me was I had my own car, and I could drive myself back to New Paltz in the morning." They climbed the steep stairs to Stefan's loft. Alma could smell the turpentine halfway up—a familiar scent, one that made her feel weak and sad. She knocked on the door and Philomena opened it.

"Oh, Alma!" she wailed, and burst into tears, flinging herself onto her daughter. Philomena's long grey hair was in a tight knot on the top of her head and fastened with two chopsticks. She was clad all in black. Black jeans, a washed-out black t-shirt, and a clunky beaded necklace, looped three times around her right wrist. "I'm sorry! I seem to have handled this all so *poorly*!" The beads rattled as she wept.

"It's okay, Mom." Alma didn't mean it, and it didn't matter. But it did put an end to Philomena's sobs. "This is Charlie Sassian."

Charlie looked a little stunned but recovered quickly. He offered Philomena his hand to shake, and she grabbed it, peering urgently into his face.

"I'm so sorry to hear about Stefan," Charlie said. "I can see he was very talented. Alma tells me he was just about to get some major press coverage. What a horrible, horrible accident."

Alma watched Charlie talk to her mother. He'd shifted into Health Department Inspector mode—professional, friendly, barely a trace of his usual self-consciousness.

"So kind of you, Charles, so kind," Philomena kept saying.

"Kind?" said Charlie, finally. "I don't know how I could have acted any other way. Toward Alma, that is. Because, well … I mean…" He was finally at a loss for words.

"Alma, Richard? This is Constance Block," said Alma's mom. "She was Stefan's agent. She'll be helping the estate, too."

The woman who nodded and stepped forward looked like she had called Philomena that morning and planned that they would wear matching outfits, except for the chopsticks. She had henna-dyed dark red hair cut in a sharp line at her shoulders and glasses with heavy black rims.

"My condolences," she said. "I know it's a sensitive situation, but Stefan must have thought quite well of you to have left you his *Dye Works* paintings," she said. "So … *civilized* of him! Have you thought about what you will be doing with the art?"

"Would a museum be interested in a donation or a loan?" said Alma. "They are, um, exquisite, of course, but…"

Philomena actually tittered, then. "My dear daughter, you do know what happens when an artist dies, don't you? An artist of your … um … *ex*-husband's stature? I know it's going to seem ghoulish…"

Ghoulish. Alma shuddered. "Stature?" she said. "I know his stuff was beginning to sell easier and there was that interview with the Times art critic."

"Precisely," said Philomena.

Constance smiled a not-so-sad smile. "He'd just hung an exhibition downtown. I've already entertained a number of offers on behalf of the estate." She patted Philomena on the arm. "There was actually a gentleman at the *wake!*"

"Collectors," said Philomena. "Since poor Stefan won't be creating any more of his wonderful paintings, the ones he left us with become more valuable."

"*Much* more valuable," said Constance. "Art is proving to be an excellent investment for people of sufficient means."

"Really?" said Alma, but she barely heard them. She watched dust dance in the sun through the big old factory windows. A shaft of light picked out the stairs to the upstairs space that had served as the bedroom. *That's where Stefan fell*, she thought, and wondered if he knew he was going to die when his foot first missed the step. She tried not to think about ghosts, but that was impossible. The studio felt empty of everything except furniture, equipment, and paintings. And dirty pots. There were plenty of those still in the kitchen sink.

A big, half-painted canvas of yet another mill town on hard times was stretched on the wall behind her mother. *That's got be somewhere in Massachusetts.* Alma remembered how often Stefan had driven up there with a camera, "stalking good decay," as he put it. There was his slide projector, across the room. That was how he made art. He blew up the photographs bigger than life and traced every wind-blown newspaper, each burned-out car. It was a painstaking process. Stefan had loved complaining about colleagues who threw paint at the canvas and got fat and rich while he labored away, trying to capture a torn curtain blowing out some empty window. Alma blinked away tears, but she wasn't sad. *I almost got stuck here. Almost.*

She examined the loft's ceiling and gazed across the room at the messy kitchen. *Stefan, are you still here, anywhere?* She couldn't help it, even though the last thing she wanted was a response. But there was no answer except a profound absence. He was really gone. And Alma wanted this meeting over.

"Alma?" That was Charlie. He slipped her a Kleenex.

"So might you be interested in putting the triptych on the market, then?" said Constance.

Alma cleared her throat. "Well, I don't exactly have any walls to hang them on at the moment," she said. *Thank God.*

"Oh, yes," said Constance. "Your mother told me all about the *tragedy* with your *flat!* So good that you had *a friend!*" She batted her eyes at Charlie and Charlie took Alma's hand. "Of course, I do understand why you chose not to attend Stefan's memorial, dear. Your mother explained to me that you're no hard-hearted Hannah. And now that I've met you, I'm sure she's right. You must know that Stefan only painted one other triptych besides the one he left you."

Actually, Alma didn't know that, but she nodded. "So, if I were to sell the Dye Works paintings…"

"Your ex-husband's other triptych went for fifty thousand," said Constance. "And that was a year ago, when he was still … alive. It will take some time for the estate to settle things, of course, but I think you will be quite pleasantly surprised."

"*Oh,*" said Alma in a small voice.

Philomena beamed. "Stefan always liked the chili at PG's in New Paltz," she said. "Shall we go have lunch and visit a little longer?"

After lunch, Charlie drove Alma's car back to Englehook. She'd driven down, but she felt a bit too flabbergasted to take the wheel on the return trip.

"Holy moly. The front end on your car is *terrible,*" he said, wallowing into the right lane. "How do you drive this thing?"

"Guess I'm used to it. Hey, it's old."

"Sounds like you could get a new one if you wanted."

"If I wanted. I don't know what I want right now."

"I know what *I* want. I was into you before you were rich."

"I'm *not* rich!" said Alma. "Not yet, anyway. I guess it's going to be pretty much money, though. This is all so *weird.* Stefan's lawyer was after me constantly and now I have a set of paintings worth *how* much?"

"Your mom said he was just trying to get you to come back to him."

"By making it so I couldn't pay my fucking bills?" Suddenly Alma was furious. "By breaking me? When he was raking in that kind of money for his paintings? Son of a bitch. I hope I get a hundred thousand on the damn triptych."

"That would be nice," said Charlie.

"It *would* be," Alma said. "Hah."

"You could go back to school. Get an MFA in poetry. And…"

"I don't know if I want that, either," said Alma. "I kind of turned myself into a cook. I just wrote my first poem in ten years. I think I like having a—I don't know—*job* job better. Maybe I'll just cook for a while and see if I keep writing. See what happens. You know what I mean?"

Charlie nodded, and signaled to pass an even more beat-up car, a primer-painted Chevy Impala the color of dirt. "By the way, the engine on this car goes like crazy. You just can't *point* it anywhere."

Alma smiled. "Ooo! Metaphor! Maybe that's what I like about it."

Charlie shook his head. "My friend Chuck on the Fire Department. He runs River Auto Repair. When stuff settles down a little, let him have a look, okay? I know what you mean about a *job* job. That's what I'm doing with the Health Department. I do something that I think helps people. Like you feeding the kids who hate the French toast. Maybe we're good people or something."

Alma gazed at Charlie. He was wearing his Irish sweater again, with a not-so-shabby tweed jacket over it. She stroked his cheek. And then she giggled.

"French toast," she said.

"Hey, happy anniversary, love," said Charlie. "We've been shacked up *a whole week*."

"One whole week? You know, it feels a lot longer," said Alma. "Which usually isn't a good thing, but in our case, I think…"

"I know what you mean," Charlie said. "It's a very good thing."

"You apparently *like* all this craziness," said Alma.

"That I do," Charlie said. "That I do."

Chapter Twenty-Eight

Thanksgiving Day

Philomena was pouring herself another glass of Beaujolais Nouveau. Alma's dad and Charlie's dad were leaning across the table, talking about how bad the economy was, and whose fault it was. They had been sparring with each other all during dinner, but they'd finally found a point of agreement—neither of them thought much of President Reagan. Charlie looked a lot like his dad, Alma thought, and wondered if he'd get that same not-quite-bald spot on the crown of his head. Charlie's mom was laughing with Mary and Cleo.

The sky over the river was just going cobalt colored.

Charlie walked into the kitchen with a stack of dirty but beautiful dinner plates, more of Aunt Eleanor's pottery. He put them down by the sink, and swept Alma up into his arms. His belly was just a little rounder than usual. But hers probably was, too. They'd both put away lots of turkey and lots of everything else. She put her arms around him.

"It worked. Nobody killed anyone," she whispered. "We all survived."

"And the stuffing was really, really good," he said. "Do we need another bottle of Beaujolais open? We're going to be into the pies in a minute."

"Yikes. My folks will probably drink it. Mom never met a food that didn't go with the vino. I'll put on water for coffee."

"Wait a minute." Charlie slipped a hand under Alma's sweater, rubbed her back and kissed her. Despite turkey and gravy and everything else, his touch was electric—a warm, comforting electricity.

"Mmmm," said Alma.

"Charlie? Do you need help out there?" That was Charlie's mom.

"No!" said Charlie. "I mean, I think I've got it under control." He kissed Alma again. "Our *next* first anniversary is coming," he said. "November 30th. One whole month. I love this."

"I love you!" said Alma. "I love that our parents are staying in a *motel!*"

"I love you, too," said Charlie. His hand slid down her back and he snapped the elastic of her underpants.

"You fresh thing!"

"This one is mine, right?" He reached around Alma to pick up a big, round glass from the counter, and swirled the wine left in it.

"Yours or maybe mine," Alma said. "Hey. We live together. Doesn't matter, y'know? Shared germs, Mr. Department of Health. Get used to it."

"Watch this," said Charlie, and drained it.

"Don't make me come out there, you two!" That was Cleo. "Where's my pie?"

"I think we need to spring into action," said Alma.

Charlie raised his eyebrows, hopefully. "*Action?*"

"*Pie* action," said Alma. She kissed his cheek and slipped out of his arms to fill the copper kettle with water for the French press pots.

"Alma," said Charlie. "I don't want to use the 'M' word yet, but I wouldn't even be surprised if we ended up—"

"Shhh!" said Alma. "Not before our second first anniversary!" Her cheeks ached. She'd come to know the feeling well. *I've been grinning like an idiot for a month.*

And that thought only made her smile more.

Outside on the front porch, where none of them could see it, a greenish light rolled itself into a sparkling globe—and floated away, across the dark Hudson River.

The End

EVERNIGHT PUBLISHING ®

www.evernightpublishing.com